PENGUIN BOOKS

Outside

Ragnar Jónasson is an international number one bestselling author who has sold over three million books in thirty-four countries worldwide. He was born in Reykjavík, Iceland, where he also works as an investment banker and teaches copyright law at Reykjavík University. He has previously worked on radio and television, including as a TV news reporter for the Icelandic National Broadcasting Service, and, from the age of seventeen, has translated fourteen of Agatha Christie's novels. He is currently writing a novel with the Icelandic Prime Minister, Katrín Jakobsdóttir. His critically acclaimed international bestseller *The Darkness* is soon to be a major TV series.

Outside

RAGNAR JÓNASSON

Translated from the Icelandic
by Victoria Cribb

PENGUIN BOOKS

PENGUIN BOOKS

UK | USA | Canada | Ireland | Australia
India | New Zealand | South Africa

Penguin Books is part of the Penguin Random House group of companies
whose addresses can be found at global.penguinrandomhouse.com

First published in Iceland with the title *Úti* by Veröld Publishing 2021
First published in Great Britain by Penguin Michael Joseph 2022
Published in Penguin Books 2022

002

Set in 12.65/14.95pt Garamond MT Std
Typeset by Jouve (UK), Milton Keynes
Printed and bound in Great Britain by Clays Ltd, Elcograf S.p.A.

The authorized representative in the EEA is Penguin Random House Ireland,
Morrison Chambers, 32 Nassau Street, Dublin D02 YH68

A CIP catalogue record for this book is available from the British Library

ISBN: 978–1–405–94910–1

This book has been translated with financial support from:

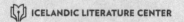

www.greenpenguin.co.uk

Penguin Random House is committed to a
sustainable future for our business, our readers
and our planet. This book is made from Forest
Stewardship Council® certified paper.

To Natalía

The snow,
mother soft,
enfolds me,
for a moment
I am saved.
I hear
a loud whisper
– are you here?
It's so cold,
hold me tight.

Fill,
fair snowdrift,
so gentle,
the emptiness
inside me,
but not quite yet . . .
. . . let me live
just a little while longer –

It was mind-numbingly cold.

Although Daníel was well bundled up in layer upon layer of wool, with a thick down jacket over the top, it didn't help: the cold still found its way inside, piercing him to the bone.

He wondered if his travelling companions were suffering similar torments but didn't dare ask in case it made him sound weak, just kept his head down and ploughed on, buffeted by the wind and driving snow. He couldn't see the surrounding landscape, couldn't tell what kind of terrain they were crossing; his whole world was reduced to a swirling whiteness and the vague shapes of figures moving ahead.

He had lost track of the time but it felt as if they had been walking for hours since the storm blew up, although probably it had been closer to an hour. No one had said anything for a while now. They were all doing their best to keep going, trying to stick close together and follow Ármann's lead. Since he knew the area better than any of them, all they could do was trust him when he said there was an old hut 'not too far away'.

The way he put it didn't exactly inspire confidence.

Despite growing up in Iceland, Daníel had been living in Britain for a number of years, first as a student at drama school, then trying to make a living on the stage.

This reunion trip with his old friends had been on the cards for a while. Ármann had offered to organize it, then, at the last minute, suggested they swap their planned visit to a holiday cottage in the south-west, within easy reach of Reykjavík, for a ptarmigan hunt in the remote highlands on the other side of the country instead. He assured them that he'd been on countless game-shooting trips in the eastern highlands and that there could be few better ways of cementing their friendship. When the message arrived, Daníel had been so busy that he simply hadn't had time to raise any objections. He didn't have a gun licence but Ármann had offered to teach him to shoot. 'There'll be no one there to see us, so you'll get a chance to bag a few birds, don't you worry.'

But as soon as they made their first foray onto the moors, everything had gone wrong.

They didn't even have their luggage with them, only provisions for that day, though they had their shotguns, of course, since that was the whole point of the exercise. Daníel had suggested leaving the guns somewhere to lighten their load and coming back for them later, but this had not gone down well.

He tried to soldier on, reminding himself that he must on no account lose his concentration. There was a tacit agreement among them to put their faith in Ármann and trust that he would get them to shelter.

Sure, Daníel was freezing, but hopefully the worst of the chill would be banished once he was safely indoors, out of the elements. He tried not to dwell on the thought that they didn't even have sleeping bags with them, and that the wretched hut they were trying to reach apparently didn't have any form of heating. No electricity; no way of getting warm. Still, at least it would provide some shelter.

As if the cold wasn't bad enough, deep down the fear was growing that they were lost; that Ármann's sense of direction wasn't all it was cracked up to be. If this turned out to be true, Daníel wouldn't just be worried, he'd be scared to death. There was no chance of their finding their way back to the lodge. If the storm continued with the same violence, they would have no choice but to stop somewhere and wait it out, but without tents or sleeping bags there was a danger they might freeze.

He couldn't see a bloody thing.

Of course, Daníel remembered storms from his youth, but nothing like this, and his years in Britain's gentler climate had softened the memories, making him forget what the cold was really like. The blizzard they were experiencing now was more brutal than he would have believed possible. And it seemed incomprehensible to him that it could be so dark in the midst of all this whirling whiteness. Could the early November dusk have fallen already? Surely they hadn't been out here that long?

He was terrified he would lose sight of the person

immediately in front of him. They were walking in more or less single file, with him bringing up the rear, and it was taking all his strength to keep up. He knew that the others were more experienced at coping with conditions like these, or at least Ármann and Helena were. They had both been eager for the hunt; not just eager but excited. Daníel had never shot a ptarmigan and now it didn't look as if the weather gods were going to give him the chance even to see one; not today, at any rate. He wasn't actually sure he'd ever tasted ptarmigan. When he was younger, perhaps.

All of a sudden, he noticed that Helena, who was second to last in the line, had stopped just in front of him. Then Daníel saw through the thickly falling flakes that the others had come to a halt. Had something happened?

Ármann called back to them but Daníel couldn't hear through his woollen hat and the thick hood of his down jacket.

Helena turned to him and said something but he still couldn't make out a word. He loosened the drawstring on his hood and pushed it back from his face.

'What did you say?' he shouted.

'Ármann says it's here, just round the corner. At least, he's pretty sure,' she said. *Pretty sure* was not what Daníel wanted to hear right now and, for the first time, as his exposed ears stung with the cold, it came home to him that they really could die of exposure out here. He could quite simply freeze to death in this snowy waste. His thoughts flew to his girlfriend in London. As far as she knew, he was on a harmless adventure tour with his Icelandic friends, though, to be fair, she had warned him against it, asking whether it wouldn't be more sensible to go on a trip like that in summer rather than in the depths of winter. She'd had a better instinct than he did for the potential hazards in his native country.

No, he mustn't think like that. He was with a good group of people and together they'd find a solution. He had to keep these negative thoughts at bay. They never did any good, as he knew from bitter experience.

He had been staring into the void, into the falling snow, but now he glanced back at Helena. She smiled at him and seemed to be waiting for him to start moving again.

'Ready?' she called.

He nodded and drew his hood back up.

The group set off again and Daníel waded through the drifts, thankful that he was wearing a good pair of boots.

But he couldn't stop his mind from conjuring up worst-case scenarios. If anything happened, he thought, if anyone got ill, they would be completely screwed. No one in the group had any medical experience.

They had each trodden their own path in life. Helena was an engineer and worked for some start-up that was making waves – according to her, anyway. Gunnlaugur was a lawyer and Ármann a guide. Well, he didn't actually want to call himself a guide any more, not since he'd set up his own tour company. These days he must be richer than all the rest of them put together. There seemed to be no let-up in the growth in tourism, and, if you believed Ármann's tall stories, he was making money off just about every visitor who came to Iceland.

Daníel liked them all well enough; that wasn't the issue. He was fond of them, in spite of their flaws. The problem was simply that whenever they met up it was generally to celebrate something – a birthday, a wedding – and on those occasions the booze always flowed freely. But he hadn't been sure he'd be able to cope with spending a whole weekend in their company, especially with no alcohol to smooth things over. He was certainly stone-cold sober now. Which was just as well, of course. But he remembered that Helena had stuck a bottle of brandy in her backpack, so at least they'd have something to warm themselves with and help calm their shattered nerves once they'd made it to the hut.

If they made it . . .

At that moment he saw a dim shape ahead.

Had they arrived?

His friends seemed to be slowing down and he allowed himself to hope.

Yes, it looked as if they'd found some sort of hut, however inadequate, out here on the wild moors.

Ármann hadn't let them down.

Daníel felt a rush of relief, as though he'd been saved from certain death. He pushed back his hood again to try to hear what the others were saying.

They were all wearing head torches and the beams darted here and there, competing to light up the hut through the driving snow. Daníel thought it was painted red, like one of the old *sæluhús*, or emergency refuges, that dotted the Icelandic highlands, but it was hard to be sure in these conditions.

Anyway, at least it was shelter from the wind and weather, which was all that mattered now.

Gunnlaugur was standing by the door and appeared to be trying to open it, but it was taking its time and Daníel could feel the cold biting harder with every second that passed.

'The door – uh – it's sticking,' Gunnlaugur called in a despairing voice. He seemed completely out of place here, battered by the savage elements.

'Let me try.' Helena pushed him aside. 'It's only locked.' Her voice was calm. It took a good deal to throw Helena off balance.

'What, locked!?' Daníel exclaimed. 'Isn't it supposed to be an emergency refuge?'

'Some huts are kept locked,' Ármann replied. 'There should be a key box here somewhere.' He directed his torch at the wall beside the door and, sure enough, there was the box, but it looked as if a code was needed to open it.

'Do you know the code?' Daníel could feel his heart beginning to pound. He had to get inside, into shelter.

'No, I don't,' Ármann said. 'I didn't know we'd be coming here. Let me think for a minute . . .'

Daníel moved closer. 'Shit. We must be able to break it open?' He took off one glove and attempted to tear the box off the wall, but it wouldn't budge and now he was acutely aware of the merciless cold. Hastily he pulled his glove back on but he'd already lost most of the feeling in his fingers. 'We need a tool of some sort.'

'Can't we just break a window?' Gunnlaugur asked, his teeth audibly chattering.

Ármann gave him a look. 'Break a window? And try to sleep in sub-zero temperatures tonight? Good luck with that . . .' His tone was acid.

'We must be able –' Gunnlaugur began, but Daníel interrupted:

'Why the hell's the hut locked? Aren't these refuges supposed to be for people in our situation? We'll die of exposure if we can't get in!'

'Calm down, Daníel,' Helena said. 'No one's going to die of exposure.'

Once again, tensions were rising among the group.

From the moment he'd stepped off the plane Daníel had started regretting his decision to take part in this weekend trip, and the feeling had grown steadily worse. He would have given anything to be at home in his little flat in London with his new girlfriend. She was an actress too, fifteen years younger than him, and, at twenty, already more successful than he was, though he wouldn't admit to this in anyone else's hearing.

'Should we try calling – try our phones?' Gunnlaugur asked.

'We're in the highlands with no signal, Gunnlaugur,' Ármann said flatly. 'We're alone here. Miles from the nearest house – the nearest person. We need to face up to the fact and sort this out ourselves. No one's coming to rescue us – or not any time soon . . .'

'It's a bloody pain that there's no phone signal here,' Daníel muttered, more to himself than to the others.

But Ármann heard and replied: 'We were aware of that. I mean, wasn't that the plan? To be in the middle of nowhere together and try to switch off for a while? That was the whole idea, wasn't it?'

Helena intervened: 'Knock it off, guys. Look, we need to open this door, then make ourselves comfortable and get some brandy down our throats. So can we concentrate, please?'

'It's a pretty flimsy door,' Gunnlaugur pointed out. 'We could probably . . .'

'We'll break open the key box. We won't do anything stupid. Then we'll buy a new box to replace it. End of story.' Ármann took the shotgun off his back.

Daníel jumped. It wasn't that he was actually expecting Ármann to shoot anyone; it was just an involuntary reaction.

'No need to worry, mate,' Ármann said with a grin, but Daníel had the odd illusion that his words were charged with meaning. There was an indefinable smell of danger in the air, among the thickly falling flakes, but he couldn't work out where it had come from. His imagination must be working overtime.

Ármann raised the butt of the gun and started hammering at the box, again and again, until it came loose, then kept on bashing at it until finally he extracted the key.

'Right,' he said. 'It worked. Now we can relax.'

This struck Daníel as grimly amusing in the circumstances. How could they relax when they were miserably cold and far from home?

Ármann put the key in the lock and, after a brief struggle to turn it, opened the door. They were met by pitch darkness.

'Well, let's get inside.'

Helena didn't wait to be told twice and almost pushed past Ármann.

Gunnlaugur followed behind, in no apparent hurry. Daníel patiently awaited his turn. At times Daníel wondered if Gunnlaugur was only half alive, he seemed so out of it.

Daníel directed his torch in front of him as he entered. It was hard to work out the size and layout of the hut with the beams of his friends' head torches flashing this way and that, criss-crossing the room.

He put down his backpack in the corner and drew a deep breath. It was chilly in here but a little warmer than it had been outside, the four walls offering a respite from the violence and screaming of the wind, and Daníel felt as if he could finally get enough oxygen in his lungs and relax a little . . .

It was then that Gunnlaugur let out a yell.

It was a piercing yell, so disturbing in the darkness and quiet that Daníel's muscles tensed in shock. After that, there was a confused noise and it took him a moment or two to work out that Gunnlaugur had cannoned into Ármann, sending them both flying.

There was a moment's deathly silence.

Daníel stood rigid with fear for several seconds, trying to work out what had happened. Gunnlaugur had seen something, that much was obvious.

'What's the matter?' he asked, but there was no reply.

Then, his limbs obeying him again, Daniel walked a little further into the hut, peering to both sides and illuminating the interior with his torch, but he couldn't see anything out of the ordinary. He shone the beam straight ahead, at the wall facing the door.

The sight that met his eyes was so unexpected, so shocking, that his heart missed a beat.

Daniel tried to cry out but couldn't utter a word, couldn't move, just stood there, staring.

He felt suddenly cold all over and the shivering spread through his body with terrifying speed.

He had never been so afraid in his life.

Friday

One day earlier

Daníel

Ármann, who had offered to drive, was the life and soul of the party as usual, doing his best to keep them entertained during the journey, but the series of amusing stories he reeled off met with indifference from his passengers. It wasn't the fault of the stories, it was just that there was a time and place for everything and this wasn't it. Daníel was dead tired as well as hung-over from the night before, and the others seemed similarly subdued. In the end, Ármann had lapsed into silence. No one else spoke, the radio was off and the only noise now was the roar of nailed tyres on the rough gravel road. Outside the windows the treeless landscape rolled past, bleak, grey and forbidding, only the high moors in the distance touched with white.

As he stared sleepily at the view, Daníel reflected how little he knew about the east of his own country. He had a hazy idea of a fjord-indented coastline and a reindeer-haunted wilderness of mountains and moors inland. A controversial hydro-electric dam. The region was associated in his mind with hardy farmers, fishermen and hunters, a world away from the urban sprawl of Reykjavík where he had grown up, though it was only about 350 kilometres as the crow flies.

They had taken it for granted that Ármann would see to everything, as always. He had shouldered responsibility for the entire organization of the trip, finding a time that suited everyone, and booking flights, a rental car and accommodation. Somehow Daníel had fallen in with all his suggestions, even the absurd idea of a ptarmigan shoot. The plan was to fly out to the east on the Friday, spend Saturday and Sunday morning shooting on the moors, then head back to town again on the Sunday evening.

They had slept off last night's pub crawl, more or less, but in spite of that Daníel hadn't felt up to doing any of the driving. He was still recovering from the bumpy flight out east in the small plane, with the bad coffee and the powerful stench of fuel, none of which had helped his hangover. Now he was sitting in the back with Helena. To give Ármann his due, he'd hired a good car; a big off-roader with plenty of leg room. The combination of a comfy seat, warm air from the heater and smooth suspension was causing Daníel's eyelids to droop. All he really wanted was to sleep until they reached their destination, as he knew that if Ármann and Helena had anything to do with it, they were bound to have another late night.

They had made the most of their evening in Reykjavík yesterday, hitting the town in style. Daníel had appreciated the chance to catch up with the latest changes, as he hadn't been home to Iceland in two years and the city had undergone a transformation in his absence. New restaurants had appeared in place of some of his old favourites and the harbour area was unrecognizable, dominated now by luxury apartments and a five-star hotel. More new hotels had opened or were about to, and the downtown area had a more cosmopolitan feel to it than ever before. He had even found a jazz bar near the parliament building, something he would have associated more with New York than Reykjavík.

The restaurant they'd chosen had been one of the recent additions, and so had the bars and clubs on their crawl, and the city centre had been buzzing for a Thursday night in November. The weather had been beautiful too, with clear skies and chilly temperatures, and the forecast was for more of the same in the east of the country over the weekend, colder though, with the possibility of a bit of precipitation thrown in.

Every time Daníel came home, he realized it took him longer to acclimatize; he found the cold a little harder to bear and had less patience with the wildly unpredictable weather. But he didn't want to risk losing face in front of the others and be told that he was going soft in the UK. In this, as in so much else, he felt his acting talents were being tested to the limit. It was vital never to let the mask fall, whether in relation to the cold or his career.

They were almost certainly under the impression that he'd hit the big time in Britain. Which was the way he wanted it. True, the drama school where he'd done his training had been a decent one, if not quite as prestigious as he implied, and after graduating he had focused on the stage and secured roles in some good plays. Few of them had made it to London, though; they were generally productions put on by touring companies doing the rounds of the provincial theatres. Still, he'd had three roles in plays in the West End; twice as an understudy – in neither case had he got to perform – and once in a walk-on role. The wages were paltry, of course, and he survived by working in restaurants on the side, but in his friends' eyes he was a star abroad, making a pretty good living. This was the role he would have to play this weekend and he didn't actually mind it that much.

'Have you really never killed anything?' It was Ármann who broke the silence.

Although Daníel knew the question was directed at him, he decided to ignore it.

'*Daníel*, have you never killed anything?' Ármann persisted.

'No, I can't see the point, to be honest,' he replied, having to raise his voice to be heard over the rumble of the tyres.

'There's something about it, you know. Something rewarding. I don't know quite how to describe it. Hunting for your own food. It makes you feel self-sufficient, in touch with nature.'

Daníel shrugged, though Ármann wouldn't be able to see as he had his eyes trained on the road ahead.

'I'm quite happy just to eat the food. That's more my scene.'

'Come on, don't be silly, you're going to shoot some birds,' Helena said, smiling at him. 'Something's got to die before we finish this trip.' Her smile held a quality he found oddly unsettling. All this talk of shooting and death had got to him, although he had been well aware that the aim of this trip was to hunt game, in addition to being a reunion, of course.

'Maybe. Sure, I'll have a go. But you'll have to keep my birds as I wouldn't dream of taking them back to England with me. I'd never get them through Customs, for one thing.'

'You wouldn't know how to cook them, anyway,' Gunnlaugur muttered, so quietly that Daníel almost missed it.

He had been rather taken aback to learn that Gunnlaugur would be joining them. He was part of the gang, of course, but in recent years, on the rare occasions they got together, there had been an unspoken agreement to leave him out. Daníel got on fine with him; after all, they'd known each other since they were kids, but Gunnlaugur didn't quite fit in. He had a placid temperament, most of the time, yet there was a darker, more difficult side to him too, as they had discovered over the years. Daníel just hoped he wouldn't display it on this trip. It wasn't as if Gunnlaugur had anything attention-grabbing to contribute to the conversation either, since his interests were limited and dull. As far as Daníel could work out, he seemed to spend most of his time alone at home watching TV.

'You don't shoot much yourself, do you, Gunnlaugur?' Daníel asked.

Gunnlaugur was never called anything else, despite being saddled with such a long name: none of the usual, affectionate short forms like 'Gulli' had ever stuck to him.

'Not really, though I'm not a bad shot,' he replied. 'Dad taught me and my brother. He taught us to fish for salmon too. As a matter of fact, it's his gun I've brought with me.'

'A trusty old friend, eh?' Helena said.

'Yes. But it's only for my use. I'm not lending it to anyone else. Just so that's clear.'

For a moment Daníel thought his old friend was joking, then he realized Gunnlaugur was deadly serious. Of course, he'd never been much of a joker.

'Keep your hair on,' Daníel said. 'No one's going to take your gun off you.'

'I only meant, seeing as you've come along without a weapon of your own.'

'I'm only –'

Helena interrupted. 'I've got a bottle of brandy with me. Ármann, you've brought some booze too, haven't you?' she asked, though she presumably knew the answer. It was a nice try at changing the subject, Daníel thought, but perhaps not the most tactful topic to bring up in the present company.

'What do you think?' Ármann grinned round at her.

Daníel leaned back and closed his eyes. If only he could have closed his ears too.

He shouldn't have let himself be talked into coming on this trip.

It was doomed to be dire. He would just have to grit his teeth and try to get through the weekend in one piece.

Gunnlaugur

'I thought you said we were staying in a hunting lodge?'

Gunnlaugur tried to keep the aggrieved note out of his voice, though he was anything but satisfied with the facilities. He wanted to let Ármann know he was unimpressed but without sounding like a whinger, so he tried to strike a bantering tone.

'Gunnlaugur, mate, this *is* a hunting lodge,' Ármann replied. 'Have you never stayed in one before?'

'Of course I have. Dad and I used to fish Haffjardará every summer. This isn't in the same class. But don't get me wrong; it's fine.' Privately, though, he felt it lacked the character of the more traditional lodges; it was all a bit too modern and soulless for him.

'Perfectly fine,' Ármann retorted.

Gunnlaugur had taken a look around inside. There were six bedrooms, all of them a bit basic, but he supposed he would just have to make the best of the situation.

They were relaxing in the living room after supper. Ármann had offered to cook that first evening, producing grilled steak and red wine to accompany the meal. Gunn-laugur had appreciated the steak, though it had been a bit overcooked, but he'd decided not to complain. He hadn't touched the wine.

His gaze was drawn to the window. It was pitch black outside and for a moment he felt a twinge of unease. Of course, he was among good friends – Daníel, Helena and Ármann were his best friends – but there was something about this place, the isolation and unrelenting darkness, that got to him. He had lost track of exactly where they were, having fallen asleep on the long drive here from the airport, and knew that, should anything go wrong, he wouldn't have a hope in hell of being able to retrace their route. The November night had made him acutely aware of how helpless he was, how totally dependent on his friends.

He had the uncanny sensation that the blackness out-side was pressing in on him. Winter trips into the highlands just weren't his thing. He preferred fishing trips in summer; standing thigh-deep in a river, wrestling with a salmon in broad daylight and decent weather. He had learned to shoot, that was no lie, but it was a long time since he had last handled a gun, and he didn't want to have to ask for help when the moment came. Didn't want to show any weakness. It would work out – it had to. After all, how difficult could it be to bag a few birds? His dad had always said that the hardest part was that first shot, feeling the kick of the gun, reconciling your-self to the act of killing. Once you'd got over that, the rest was easy.

'How on earth did you find this place?' he asked.

Ármann gave him a look and took a sip of his drink. He was on gin and tonic, like Helena and Daníel. Gunnlaugur was sticking to soda water.

'This place?'

'I mean the lodge.'

'I worked out here in the east for two years. I know it very well. After all, I've dragged enough tourists round these parts. That's how I started the company, by –'

Gunnlaugur cut him short. 'We're in good hands, then.' He'd heard this story too many times, in one form or another. How a small-scale operation in the east of Iceland, *the germ of an idea*, as Ármann sometimes described it, had grown into a company with what must be a turnover of several hundred million krónur. Maybe even a billion? Gunnlaugur had no interest in dwelling on the figures or on Ármann's success. He himself had slogged through a law degree, not out of any particular interest or aptitude, but only because he had twice failed his medical exams. At that point his dad had told him enough was enough and he should give law a go instead. He had only failed one of his exams on that course, and scraped through his degree somehow. For the last few years he had been working for a medium-sized law firm in Reykjavík, every day the same as the last. There was enough to do and he wasn't always bored, but it was hard to watch his younger colleagues surging ahead, while he was left behind, stuck in the same rut. All his grafting had earned him was a small house and a car. Ármann, on the other hand, without a qualification to his name, was raking in money at such a rate that Gunnlaugur knew he would never be able to catch up. Not unless Ármann somehow managed to blow the lot. Gunnlaugur was fond of Ármann, but sometimes, after being forced to listen to his endless boasting, he found himself uncharitably hoping that there would be another financial crisis, of some kind or another, and that the tour company would go bust . . . Then the cards could be dealt out again and perhaps he himself would get a better hand this time.

'How's your love life?' Helena asked. She was in the habit of asking him this every time they met, probably because he had proved so hopeless at holding on to girlfriends over the years. He wasn't that bad-looking but somehow his relationships never lasted beyond a few weeks. He had been more successful abroad, during his time as an exchange student in Denmark, where he had met a girl who had stayed with him for four whole months. And of course he'd always had a thing for Helena. She was well aware of the fact too, though they'd never discussed it and it would almost certainly never come to anything. No doubt that was why she enjoyed teasing him about his love life.

'I'm not seeing anyone at the moment,' he said, striving to sound casual. Determined not to let it get to him. 'How about you?'

Helena smiled coolly.

None of your bloody business was the answer he read from her expression.

'Have we finished the lot?' Daníel waved his empty glass. 'Ármann, you're on bar duty this evening.'

Ármann got to his feet.

'This is such a bad idea,' Gunnlaugur blurted out, sighing heavily. The wind had picked up outside and even in his thick woollen jumper he was feeling the cold.

Helena looked at him. 'What?'

'Oh, sorry, I just meant coming here. We're stuck in the middle of nowhere, lucky to have electricity and heating, but if anything happened, you know . . . If we . . .'

'What could possibly happen?' Daníel asked, still holding out his empty glass, waiting for Ármann to play waiter.

'I don't know,' Gunnlaugur replied. 'Anything . . . If we couldn't get back, for example . . .' He felt his claustrophobia flaring up at the thought. 'If we were forced to walk . . .'

'We won't have to walk back,' Helena said. 'Don't be silly, Gunnlaugur.'

'I just meant, if the jeep broke down, we could all die of exposure,' he said, then immediately regretted his choice of words. Silence descended on the three of them sitting around the coffee table. Ármann had gone into the kitchen, so perhaps he had missed the last remark.

Gunnlaugur met his friends' eyes, first Helena's, then Daníel's. Neither said a word. He knew it was his fault. He had a habit of doing this, of just coming out with stuff, not stopping to think before he opened his mouth. It was a singularly inappropriate subject to raise among this particular group of friends.

It occurred to him to apologize and take it back, but he couldn't find the right words, and at that moment Ármann reappeared with the gin bottle in one hand and the tonic in the other.

'Refill?' he asked, as cheerful and easy-going as ever.

'Now you're talking,' Daníel said, holding out his glass.

'Yes, please,' Helena said, her voice unusually colourless. Gunnlaugur's foot-in-mouth comment must have got to her.

Ármann went over to her and mixed the drink like a professional bartender.

He was on his way back into the kitchen when Gunnlaugur called out to him. It wasn't a conscious decision but he said it anyway. 'Have you got a glass for me?' The moment the words were out, he wished he could take them back. He was feeling ill at ease and the oppressive sense of isolation wasn't helping. Maybe everything would be that bit more bearable if only he had a drink inside him. Just a tiny one. 'Not too strong, though,' he added, as if that would mitigate his decision.

Ármann stopped and turned sharply. His expression suggested he thought he must have misheard.

'A glass for you, Gunnlaugur?' he asked after a pause, his voice carefully neutral.

'Yes,' Gunnlaugur replied, a little uncertainly, though he knew deep down that there was no going back now. He could already anticipate the bitter taste tingling on his tongue.

'A glass for Gunnlaugur,' Ármann said lightly, as though nothing could be more natural. Putting the bottles down on the table, he went into the kitchen and came straight back with another glass. 'I'll leave you to mix it,' he said.

Gunnlaugur knew this was deliberate. It gave him one last chance to change his mind. That way the responsibility would be his alone and nothing to do with his friends.

He served himself, making sure to add a generous slug of gin.

Then he raised the glass to his lips, inhaling the aroma, the blissful feeling of anticipation stealing through his body.

And took his first drink for two years.

Helena

It had taken Helena a while to drop off. It had been past one by the time she went to her room, leaving the boys still hard at it, and she had reminded them that if the plan was to go out and shoot some ptarmigan in the morning, it would be as well to get a good night's sleep.

She had been taken aback to see Gunnlaugur drinking, since, as far as she knew, he had been sober for ages. Booze didn't agree with him, as no one who knew him could have failed to notice.

Waking with a jolt, she opened her eyes. In the impenetrable blackness she couldn't work out what it was that had disturbed her or how long she had been asleep. All she was aware of was a feeling of disquiet. She closed her eyes again and drew a deep breath.

It came back to her that she had been dreaming, yet again, about Víkingur. Five years had passed and yet he still visited her most nights. The dreams were always a little vague but the impression they left behind was warm.

Contentment, happiness even, but no sorrow – not until she woke up to that terrible sense of desolation.

Five years and she was still on her own. She'd had the odd lover in the meantime but nothing that had lasted. It was as if she entered into every relationship having already decided that no one could live up to Víkingur. And she was on her own at present.

She turned over onto her side. It was chilly in the room, in cruel contrast to the warmth of her dream. She hoped she would be able to go straight back to sleep and maybe find her way back to Víkingur, but generally when she woke up in the middle of the night like this she had trouble dropping off again and, if sleep did come, it tended to be dreamless.

God, how she missed him . . .

'Helena.'

She started. She could have sworn she'd heard a voice whispering her name. Her heart beating faster, she sat up. Her eyes took a moment or two to adjust to the darkness, but then she saw that there was someone in the room, a shadowy figure over by the door, gradually moving towards her. She stiffened with fear, unable to speak, the words caught in her throat. It might have been better to get out of bed but she couldn't move.

'Helena,' came the whisper again, slightly louder this time.

'Who . . . who is it?' she asked, keeping her voice down. She didn't know what was stopping her from shouting the question at the top of her voice.

'Helena, don't be scared. It's only me.'

In that instant, it dawned on her who it was. Dread started coursing through her body like poison. Although she had been feeling a little drunk when she went to bed, she was fully alert now and stone-cold sober. Her visitor, on the other hand, sounded pretty wrecked, judging by the way he was slurring.

'It's me, Gunnlaugur.'

'What are you doing? Are you out of your mind?' she hissed, still without raising her voice.

'I . . . I just wanted to check on you,' he said, closer now. His voice was thick; his breath reeked of spirits.

He sat down heavily on her bed, making it almost impossible for her to get up. She remained where she was, clutching the duvet around her.

'I just . . . I was just thinking, you know . . .'

'No, Gunnlaugur, I don't know. I was asleep. Can you go away, please? Now.'

'I'm going, I'm going. I just wanted to check on you. I got the idea – from what you said earlier – that you're alone these days. No boyfriend.'

His dark shadow loomed towards her.

'Get out. It's never going to happen.'

At that, Gunnlaugur rose unsteadily to his feet and took a step or two backwards, then paused, still uncomfortably close.

'I . . . I just, you know, we're both on our own and it's cold . . . I thought we could, you know, warm each other up a bit . . .'

'Gunnlaugur, just go to bed.' And *stop drinking*, she added under her breath.

He stood there, swaying a little, but going nowhere. Her eyes had adjusted better now and although she was still clutching the duvet she was no longer scared, exactly. She reckoned she was probably more than a match for Gunnlaugur in his current state, but she was equally confident that she could persuade him to leave without it coming to a struggle. If all else failed, she could shout out to Ármann. He was in the next-door room and the walls were thin.

'Will you get out?' she said, raising her voice a little.

To her relief, he started backing away.

'Out, now, Gunnlaugur. Go to bed. Stop behaving like an idiot.'

'You know we'd be good together, Helena,' he said, breathing heavily. 'You know that.' Then he seemed to change his mind and before she knew it he was moving swiftly towards her. Stooping over her, he started kissing her on the mouth.

She wrenched her head away and gave him a violent shove, yelling: 'For fuck's sake, Gunnlaugur, get out!'

He toppled over onto the floor with a crash.

Ármann

Ármann jerked awake. He'd only just dropped off when Helena's yell disturbed him.

What the fuck? he thought, leaping out of bed.

She was in the room next door, just like old times.

Rushing out into the hallway, he saw in the gloom that her door was ajar. He switched on the light and got a shock when he was presented with the sight of Gunnlaugur sprawled on the floor. Helena climbed out of bed, looking dazed and blinking in the sudden brightness, but there was a flash of fury in her eyes. He recognized that expression only too well.

'What the hell's going on?' Ármann asked sharply, directing his words at the man on the floor. Gunnlaugur didn't answer, just made a feeble effort to sit up.

'Are you all right?' Ármann asked Helena, the concern clear in his voice.

She nodded.

'What happened?'

She didn't immediately answer, taking a moment to consider, to formulate her reply. That was Helena all over.

'Gunnlaugur got the wrong room,' she said at last.

'The wrong room?' Ármann could see that she was holding something back. 'Gunnlaugur, get up! What's going on?'

Gunnlaugur finally managed to recover enough to clamber to his feet.

'I . . . I, yeah, I just came into her room by accident . . . Sorry . . .'

'And what? What happened?' Ármann turned to Helena. 'Why did you yell like that?'

She didn't answer.

Ármann went right up to Gunnlaugur, who was standing there, swaying slightly.

'Gunnlaugur.' Ármann's voice was level but he had got his friend's attention. He locked eyes with him. 'What were you doing in here?'

Gunnlaugur's gaze wandered hazily to Helena, then back to Ármann.

'Sorry,' he muttered indistinctly. 'Just need to go to bed.'

'What the hell were you thinking of, to start drinking again this evening?'

'I . . . I don't know. Don't hurt me . . .'

Ármann backed away, a little disconcerted. 'What? You think I'm going to hurt you? Who the hell do you think I am? Were you trying it on with Helena? Tell me the truth.'

'No . . . No, I didn't do anything. I . . .'

'Helena?' Ármann caught and held her gaze. 'Is there something you want to tell me? We can go straight back to town, if you like. Give up on the whole thing. If that's what you want?'

'Don't be ridiculous, Ármann. It's all right. You know what he's like when he's been drinking.'

Ármann nodded and turned back to Gunnlaugur. 'Watch it, you.'

'Yes,' Gunnlaugur replied, in a low, pathetic voice.

'Behave yourself, OK?'

'OK.'

'You'd better not drink any more on this trip. There are guns in the house. We all need clear heads.'

'OK,' Gunnlaugur muttered again, then made to squeeze past Ármann, out of the room.

Ármann stood his ground, making no attempt to step out of the way, but didn't say another word. He was sure something more had happened and that Helena was covering for Gunnlaugur because she wanted to avoid upsetting their plans at the very outset of the trip. It was no secret that Gunnlaugur had a drink problem. There had been times in the old days when he'd been seriously out of order, becoming extremely unpleasant, even aggressive, when drunk. The problem had escalated until finally he had got a grip on himself and quit. As they didn't really stay in touch these days, Ármann didn't know how long he had been on the wagon, but it had come as a shock when Gunnlaugur had asked for a gin and tonic earlier that evening.

'Helena?' Ármann said quietly, once Gunnlaugur had gone.

She just looked at him in silence. They understood each other, without need of words.

'Go back to sleep,' he said gently. 'It's all going to be fine.'

Saturday

Daníel

'Right, have you got everything I told you to bring?' Ármann asked.

He was standing in the doorway. Daníel had lined up his things on the bed, ready to put in his backpack.

'I think so,' he replied, a little hesitantly, hoping his voice wouldn't betray his doubts. He had been dragged out of bed bright and early, though he would have preferred a lie-in after the heavy session yesterday evening, but he felt surprisingly chirpy, considering. He'd been woken by some disturbance during the night but had turned over and gone back to sleep. He couldn't work out what had happened, though Gunnlaugur had been looking noticeably sorry for himself at breakfast. Ármann had taken responsibility for the catering again; their self-appointed guide – or travel expert, as he would no doubt have put it himself. Toast and bacon, not bad at all; a bit of fuel in the belly to kick-start the day.

'Head torch?'

Daníel looked momentarily blank. 'Er, yes.' He surveyed

the items laid out on his bed, unable to see it anywhere, though he definitely remembered buying one in London.

'You know, you could die without it, Daníel. If you lose us and it starts to get dark . . .'

Daníel felt his trepidation stirring again but tried to ignore it. 'I know it's here somewhere . . .' He rooted around in his backpack and finally found it. 'But I'm not planning on leaving your sides for a minute – I'd be totally helpless without you.'

'Don't worry, mate. We'll look after you. I'll lend you a gun. Trust me, you'll enjoy it.'

Although Daníel had his doubts about that, he tried to look on the bright side. If nothing else, this would be an adventure. He reminded himself that it was good to collect experiences for later use, to extend his repertoire as an actor. One of these days his career would take off, he had to believe that, and then it would be useful to know what it felt like to do battle with the forces of nature.

'What's the forecast like?' he asked.

'It was all right last time I checked, but obviously we haven't got a phone signal here. Since we're going to have to walk a fair way and gain some height to get up to the snowline, we can't expect conditions to be any better than they are now. We'll just have to cope, Daníel.' Ármann grinned.

'And you're absolutely sure you know the way? I wouldn't want to get lost . . .'

'Of course. I'm in my element out here,' Ármann replied airily. 'It's how I make my living, remember? I wouldn't have been able to build up an empire like mine if I didn't know what I was doing.'

Here we go, Daníel thought to himself. Yet another reminder of how well Ármann was doing, how much money he was making. Daníel put it down to a raging inferiority complex that meant Ármann constantly felt the need to prove himself. To be honest, Daníel had never really believed his friend would amount to anything. Ármann had been constantly in trouble at school, had never been very academic, and afterwards he had gone spectacularly off the rails, getting mixed up in drugs and dodgy company. He didn't have looks on his side either, though of course one shouldn't judge a person purely on that basis. Daníel, in contrast, had always been considered the best-looking guy in their circle of friends and he was well aware of the fact; people had always been drawn to him. Ármann had had a long-term girlfriend but didn't have any kids, and he'd been single since his relationship ended. These days he gave the impression of being married to his job.

'Good for you,' Daníel replied amiably. 'For getting such a handle on the tourist business. I'll bear that in mind when I come over to Iceland on location, as obviously we'll need a tour operator to take us around the country.' He couldn't resist the temptation to paint a much brighter picture of his career than the reality warranted.

'Oh, really? You've got a role in a film shooting in Iceland?' There was a hint of mockery in Ármann's voice that Daníel couldn't miss. Perhaps it had been intentional.

'It's in negotiation, yeah, though I can't really discuss it at this stage. I've got a number of projects on the go – you know how it is.' It wasn't even a white lie: the only projects Daníel was currently juggling were the role of understudy in a play that would be performed in a few provincial theatres around Britain at Christmas and some auditions at the beginning of December.

'Well, I look forward to seeing it. Will it be shown in cinemas or online?'

'Too early to say,' Daníel replied, deliberately vague, eager to change the subject. 'By the way, I brought along a newspaper, like you asked, though I can't imagine why that was on the list you sent me. Yesterday's copy of *The Times*, bought at the airport. Though I don't quite understand. Are you planning to read it?'

Ármann laughed. 'I don't read the papers,' he answered, then seemingly couldn't resist adding: 'Unless I'm in them. Or one of my companies is advertising.'

Yet again, his inability to pass up a chance to brag set Daníel's teeth on edge. 'Right, well, I'll just throw it away, then,' he said.

'Whoa, hold your horses! You need to bring it with you. The rest of us have our own. If you shoot a bird – *when* you shoot a bird – make sure you wrap it in a double-page spread before you put it in your backpack. That way the newspaper will sop up the blood.'

Daníel nodded and pulled on his blue down jacket, shuddering slightly at the thought.

'We brought along a packed lunch for you, as promised,' Ármann went on. 'Hearty Icelandic fare: dried fish and liver sausage. And an empty water bottle. Helena's got a bottle of brandy in her rucksack too, in case anyone gets cold.'

'An empty water bottle . . . ?'

'To fill from a stream, of course.'

Ármann gave him a heavy slap on the back. 'Excited, Daníel? You won't experience anything like this in London. Pure nature, the merciless elements: it doesn't get any better than that. Life's no fun unless you challenge yourself from time to time. I'm proud of you.'

'We'll try and have a good time,' Daníel replied, and started stuffing items into his pack.

Brandy in Helena's rucksack, Ármann had said . . . Booze and guns . . . That couldn't be a good combination, particularly in light of the odd undercurrents that he was sometimes aware of within their group.

He just had to cling to the belief that it would all turn out fine in the end.

Gunnlaugur

'I've been poring over maps to find the best areas, trust me,' Ármann said as they set off. Gunnlaugur tried to listen but he couldn't focus on the words; they just echoed somewhere in the back of his head. He was feeling horrible, both mentally and physically, after last night. The persistent headache reminded him what a terrible idea it had been to have a drink, and yet what he wouldn't have given for a beer now – just a small pick-me-up.

He couldn't recall exactly what had happened between him and Helena in the night. Snatches of memory came back to him: he'd been in her room, spoken to her, fallen over, seen Ármann, but when he woke up this morning he'd been lying on the floor of his own room. He hoped to God he'd behaved himself but had nagging doubts on that score. He hadn't exchanged a word with Helena or Ármann so far today, having deliberately turned up late to breakfast and avoided lingering long at the table. Although the atmosphere had been noticeably strained, he got the impression they'd made up their minds not to let him ruin the trip. In a way it was a relief, as he wouldn't have wanted that on his conscience, but at the same time he felt a strong desire to vanish off the face of the earth. If only he could go home, crawl into bed and get some more sleep.

'This should be a laugh,' Daníel said, slapping Gunnlaugur matily on the shoulder. His words rang a bit hollow but Gunnlaugur smiled. At least Daníel hadn't stopped talking to him, like the other two. Could he have overheard what happened in the night? Gunnlaugur sincerely hoped not.

'Yes, sure. I'll have to teach you how to handle a gun,' Gunnlaugur replied, tentatively entering into the spirit of things. It was nippy out here and with some luck the fresh air would help revive him. Like the others, he was well equipped for the weather. Only Daníel gave him cause for concern: his down jacket looked a bit light-weight. He'd probably bought it from some luxury outfitters in London where people weren't prepared for the extreme conditions you could expect in Iceland. Not that Gunnlaugur really cared if Daníel put designer labels before survival. It was none of his business. He thought sourly that it would be typical of Daníel to prize looks over substance; for him, appearances were everything.

Gunnlaugur had made a big deal at the office about the fact he was going on a shoot with his friends. His colleagues had expressed surprise: they hadn't had him down as the type to enjoy hunting ptarmigan, and, come to think of it, they probably hadn't believed he had any friends either. After all, he didn't usually spend much time chatting to people at work, preferring to keep himself to himself.

He had been hoping the weekend would give him a chance to forget about the tedium of his caseload and the way the partners at the firm treated him like a workhorse. Subconsciously, he had probably also been dreaming of Helena. Although he supposed he had always known that nothing would come of his crush on her, last night the gin had almost caused him to step off a cliff.

He was going to quit drinking – again.

And do his best to enjoy the weekend, as far as humanly possible.

Helena

Helena drew the bitterly cold air deep into her lungs, feeling exhilarated as the oxygen flowed through her body. She surveyed the view, trying to savour the moment and the stark beauty of the landscape unfolding around them. For most of the morning they had been trekking over a harsh, monotonous terrain of gravel and rock, enlivened only by patches of icy moss, but now they had climbed up as far as the snowline and the high moors gleamed white ahead, as far as the eye could see.

Last night she had come so close to letting Gunnlaugur wreck the trip. She'd seriously considered packing her bags and going home; all their plans ruined.

She was sure that Ármann had been thinking the same thing; she'd read it in his face.

Then she had come to her senses. It wasn't the first time Gunnlaugur had behaved like an idiot, though he'd never hit on her that aggressively before. In normal circumstances she would have stormed off, but that was easier said than done out here. It would have meant the

49

whole group having to go home, since they only had the one car.

She'd breakfasted early, gambling on the likelihood that Gunnlaugur would be among the latecomers, which had proved the case. They hadn't exchanged a word so far this morning; she'd avoided even looking his way. She hadn't the slightest interest in any further interaction with him, but of course that would be difficult to keep up all weekend.

He'd always been a pain in the neck. In fact, it was surprising he'd ever become part of their circle of friends. He and Daníel had been in the same class at school and later both went on to the Commercial College, where Gunnlaugur had clung to Daníel and his friends as if he had no other mates there, which was probably true. For some reason they had felt sorry for him and admitted him to their gang. Basically, it was all Daníel's fault. He would do anything to avoid confrontation and just seemed happy to accept that people wanted to hang around with him.

After they had been going for a couple of hours, they stopped for a breather and perched on some bare rocks to eat their packed lunches. Helena was wryly amused when she saw Daníel's expression as he inspected the traditional delicacies. He'd obviously got out of the habit of eating dried fish during his years in London.

Her gaze shifted to their surroundings. The snow looked old. It was thin and patchy where it had melted in the days since it had fallen. With any luck this would make it easier to spot the ptarmigan, since their white winter plumage would stand out starkly against the areas of dark stony ground.

After a brief lunchbreak they moved on again, as it was too chilly to sit around for long. Another hour or so passed, the group trudging along mostly without talking, Gunnlaugur and Daníel looking as if they needed to conserve their breath. Helena began to wonder if they were ever going to find any birds. The moors stretched out on every side, vast, treeless and silent. They hadn't seen a single sign of life since leaving the lodge that morning.

Helena frowned, her gaze lingering on the thick pall of cloud building up on the horizon. It looked a lot more ominous than forecast, but the organization of the trip was entirely in Ármann's hands and she trusted him. The wind wasn't supposed to pick up until evening and by then they would be safely in shelter.

'Are you sure there are ptarmigan here?' Daníel asked, eventually breaking the silence.

Ármann came to a halt, his breath forming clouds as he spoke. 'It's all a question of patience, persistence and reading the landscape. We need to climb up a bit higher to find the right habitat but the conditions are perfect: dry and windless.'

'And bloody cold,' Daníel retorted.

'As a matter of fact, that's excellent,' Ármann said. 'The colder, the better. Minus five and below is ideal because they stay sitting for longer and fly shorter distances.'

The temperature didn't bother Helena. As a rule, she relished the cold.

'What are those tracks?' Daníel asked.

Ármann looked down at the line of paw prints crossing their path. 'Fox. We won't see any, though. They'll steer well clear of us.'

'Oh, OK. So, let's keep going, then,' Daníel said.

Helena could have sworn there was a faint tremor in his voice. Was he afraid? If so, what of?

Ármann

It wasn't supposed to snow. Not immediately. Yet, out of nowhere, a blizzard had blown up.

The afternoon hadn't been going as well as he had hoped. Everything had been fine this morning: they had climbed up to the snowline and paused for a bite to eat on the edge of the moors, full of anticipation at the thought of a good day's shooting, but after that they had slogged for hours over desolate, featureless terrain without seeing so much as a single bloody bird. Ármann had been on his mettle, keen to show off his prowess as a guide, but instead he had become increasingly aware of the others' frustration, as every time he promised that they were approaching a likely spot the ptarmigan failed to appear. He and Helena kept having to stop and wait for Gunnlaugur and Daníel, who toiled, panting, in their wake, looking ever more dispirited. Tempers among the group were beginning to fray and Ármann knew he was losing their confidence. Even Helena was silent at his side.

He had been uneasily aware of the clouds piling up on

the horizon but put his faith in the weather forecast and stuck to the route he had planned. The change, when it came, was terrifyingly sudden. A squall of wind came whistling over the icy ground, bringing them to a standstill with the shock of its force. Next minute, black clouds were rolling towards them at an unbelievable pace, obliterating the sky and filling the air with blinding pellets of snow.

Ármann tried to stay calm. The whiteout had come like a bolt from the blue, but of course he should have known that the weather in the highlands was unpredictable all year round, and especially in November.

Shit.

The others were standing in a huddle, pulling up their hoods and trying to keep their balance against the buffeting of the wind. He felt they were looking to him for guidance, though he couldn't make out their faces through the stinging flakes. In normal conditions he would have no trouble finding the hut, but he had to admit to himself, although he would never do so to the others, that this unexpected blizzard wasn't going to make his job easy.

'We'd better hang on here for a bit,' he called, going over to join them, hoping his words wouldn't be drowned out by the roaring of the gale.

He heard Helena shout back, 'OK!'

'Not for long,' he added. 'Maybe five, ten minutes, and see if it passes over.'

No sooner had he spoken than he realized this was a bad idea. Now that they had stopped moving, the knife-edged wind cut right through their clothes. They would have to keep walking if they weren't to freeze.

He knew his way to the hut from here. He was sure of it. It was just easier when visibility wasn't reduced to a few metres.

'What's going on?' Gunnlaugur demanded. 'I thought we'd checked the forecast?'

Not for the first time, Gunnlaugur was getting on Ármann's nerves. But he couldn't remember ever having been this fed up with him before. Gunnlaugur had made such an idiot of himself last night that they should have sent him packing. He'd been suitably chastened this morning, but Ármann hoped he wasn't going to start acting up now.

'Gunnlaugur!' he shouted, allowing his irritation to break through. 'You're welcome to go back now if you want.' Ármann stood there, without moving, glaring at his supposed friend.

'What? Oh no, I'm not going anywhere. There's nowhere for me to go.' Gunnlaugur swung his head from side to side, as if he were actually seeking an escape route.

'Exactly, there's nowhere for you to go, Gunnlaugur. We're all in this together, whether we like it or not.' They hadn't shot a single bird, but right now Ármann couldn't give a damn about that. He would just have to guide them to the little hut. In good weather it was probably half an hour's walk from here, but he couldn't guess how long it would take them with the snow coming down this heavily. One hour – two, maybe? Assuming he managed to lead them there at the first attempt . . .

Daníel

Daníel stumbled over the rough ground, battling against the force of the wind, afraid of losing sight of the others, because if he did, he knew he was unlikely to survive.

He could dimly see their shapes ahead through the driving sheets of white: Gunnlaugur, Ármann and Helena.

He remembered his introduction to Ármann and Helena so well. It had been his first day at the Commercial College and he'd meant to turn up early to bag the best seat, in the corner at the back. He didn't know many people at the college but was following in the footsteps of his parents, who had met there and then gone on to set up their own company. The only person who had come with him from his old school was Gunnlaugur. They'd been in the same class for ten years and Daníel was resigned to having to spend time with him, although he'd never particularly liked him. The ties were simply too strong after all these years for him to ditch Gunnlaugur that easily.

That first day at college was still vivid in his mind's eye. Ármann and Helena had been sitting in the corner at the back of the classroom, just where he had been intending to park himself. Spotting a free seat beside them, he had taken it, smiling, and introduced himself. Their conversation had been a little constrained and self-conscious that first day, but it had quickly become easier and soon they'd struck up a friendship. By choosing to join them, Daníel had succeeded in killing two birds with one stone, since it meant Gunnlaugur couldn't sit beside him. In the event, Gunnlaugur had turned up late and been forced to take a seat at the front, practically at the teacher's desk. Since no one had claimed the seat beside him, Gunnlaugur had been free to keep all his pens and pencils to himself. As Daníel knew, there was little Gunnlaugur disliked more than sharing his belongings with other people. He'd been like that at six years old and hadn't changed one bit.

After college, they had all gone down separate paths: Gunnlaugur to study first medicine, then law, and Helena engineering. They'd always been the best students in the group. Daníel had headed to Britain to realize his dream of becoming an actor. Those had been the best years of his life, better even than at the Commercial College; the whole world open to him, all those opportunities within reach. But the older he got, the more he found the doors closing. After drama school, he had moved home and worked for a while in Icelandic theatres. Then he'd gone abroad again, gambling everything on this chance to get his breakthrough and hit the big time. He'd had a handful of opportunities, though never anything that got him noticed, but he'd kept on grafting until it was too late to turn back. It felt like being in a casino where he kept putting all his chips on the same number, which stubbornly refused to come up. So far, at any rate. At some point his parents had said it was time he grew up and took responsibility for his future. He had taken it badly at the time, but of course he knew what they meant. He was renting a small flat in the East End of London, scraping to make ends meet every month, and had a quick turnover of girlfriends, the latest of whom was only just twenty. The truth was that he owned almost nothing and in that sense he envied his friends.

Yet, like Helena and Gunnlaugur, Daníel had made far more sensible decisions after leaving school than Ármann had.

As he struggled gamely after the others, a visitor in his own country, he was aware of a churning sense of envy.

And it was directed almost entirely towards Ármann.

Helena

She had noticed the slight hesitation, as if Ármann wasn't quite sure they were going the right way. He disguised it well, though, and she was sure neither of the others had picked up on it. But then no one knew him as well as she did.

She had complete faith in him. Probably more than he had in himself, and perhaps it had always been that way. Whenever he wavered, she had been the one who set him in motion again.

Ármann could be trusted to save the day.

Yet it wasn't that long ago that she'd had to save him from himself. He'd moved to Denmark after leaving college, intending to work for a year or two to save up some money. As time went by, she'd had less and less contact with him. At twenty-two he was still in Denmark, still without a proper job, so it hadn't come as any great surprise to Helena when she heard that he'd been sucked into the world of drugs, first as a user, then as a dealer.

He had always been reckless. The susceptible type.

And she had always taken care of him, helping him with his schoolwork, trying to keep him on the straight and narrow, until he had moved to Copenhagen, out of her reach. She had gone over there more than once with the idea of fetching him home, but it hadn't worked. Then had come the momentous phone call that had, ironically enough, ended up turning his life around.

Ármann had broken his leg. He'd fallen downstairs was the story she was fed. She never asked him what had happened, not wanting to know if it had really been an accident or something more sinister, like a fight or a beating by debt-collectors. All that really mattered was that Ármann had come home to Iceland and managed, slowly but surely, to get back on his feet, in more senses than one.

He was a powerful ally but a bad enemy. If you got on the wrong side of him, you'd better watch out.

Gunnlaugur

There were times when Gunnlaugur felt like an onlooker in life rather than a participant. Sure, he had enough to keep him busy during the day, but his job was monotonous and he couldn't see himself performing either well enough to be promoted or badly enough to be sacked. When he stopped to think about it, though, perhaps being fired wouldn't be so bad; it might shake him up a bit. Force him into movement again, out of his rut. Because he knew he would never quit his job on his own initiative: that would be too risky. What if he couldn't find a position anywhere else? A few months without pay and he might have to go crawling to Ármann and beg him for work . . . But would Ármann say yes? There was no guarantee.

Gunnlaugur clung to his small circle of old friends. This group was it, basically, his only friends, but they never got in touch unless they needed legal advice or it was one of those few occasions when they felt they had to invite him along out of a sense of duty.

That was why he had let himself be talked into coming

on this shooting trip, bringing along his dad's old shotgun but not a lot of courage. And now it was as if the weather gods had decided to punish the group, and him as well. He would have given anything to be relaxing at home, despite the lack of company there. Even his solitary existence was better than being stuck in the middle of the highlands in a snowstorm. And even if Ármann managed to find the hut he had mentioned, Gunnlaugur didn't exactly relish the thought of spending the night there, forced to sleep in primitive, cramped conditions with his friends. Especially not after what had happened last night . . .

At that point the horrible thought crossed his mind that it might not be just one night: storms could rage for days out here.

It was then that Ármann came to a halt.

'It's here, just over the hill!' he shouted above the wind. 'I'm pretty sure.'

Gunnlaugur peered round at Helena and Daníel. They both stopped and seemed to exchange a few words.

Ármann set off again, shoulders hunched against the weather, Gunnlaugur following close on his heels, thanking God they would soon be in shelter.

It wasn't long before the refuge appeared. Gunnlaugur had never been so relieved to see a building before. Picking up his pace, he overtook Ármann and reached the hut first, and immediately tried to open the door, only to find that it wouldn't budge.

'Can't we just break a window?' he asked, after they had tried in vain for a while to find a way in. He was so unspeakably cold that his teeth were chattering.

'Break a window?' Ármann said. 'And try to sleep in sub-zero temperatures tonight? Good luck with that . . .'

Gunnlaugur tried to calm down and hang on to his composure. He asked instead if they should try their phones but this suggestion was given equally short shrift.

'We'll break open the key box. We won't do anything stupid. Then we'll buy a new box to replace it. End of story,' Ármann said, after a bit of an argument. He took the shotgun off his back and battered the box with the butt until it came off the wall.

After they had managed to open the door, Gunnlaugur followed Helena and Ármann inside. Daníel was behind him.

Gunnlaugur flashed his torch around, trying to get a sense of the interior, but when his eyes followed its beam to the corner at the back, what he saw made him cry out in shock. Stumbling sideways in the gloom, he collided with Ármann and sent them both crashing to the floor.

Daníel

There was a moment's deathly silence.

He stood rigid with fear for several seconds, trying to work out what had happened. Gunnlaugur had seen something, that much was obvious.

Then, his limbs obeying him again, Daníel walked a little further into the hut, peering to both sides and illuminating the interior with his torch, but he couldn't see anything out of the ordinary. He shone the beam straight ahead, at the wall facing the door.

The sight that met his eyes was so unexpected, so shocking, that his heart missed a beat.

He tried to cry out but couldn't utter a word, couldn't move, just stood there, staring.

He felt suddenly cold all over and the shivering spread through his body with terrifying speed.

He had never been so afraid in his life.

Daníel stumbled backwards, they all did, and after a moment of confused jostling they were standing outside the hut again, buffeted by the wind, back in the merciless, bone-piercing cold.

'What . . . what the hell was that?' Daníel finally managed to stammer. He was shaking so badly he could barely get the words out. 'What the hell . . . ?'

His gaze swung round Ármann, Helena and Gunnlaugur, searching their faces.

Had he been seeing things? Perhaps it had been an illusion caused by the extreme conditions. He was in such a state, mentally and physically exhausted after battling with the elements, that his eyes must have deceived him. That was the only explanation that made any sense.

Yet . . . yet they had all been equally shocked. And he could sense their fear and doubt as they stood there outside the hut, the snow collecting on their clothes again, nobody saying a word. The seconds seemed to pass in slow motion, so slowly that he wanted to scream, at the sky and the wind-driven snow that was screeching so savagely back at him.

At that moment he would have given anything to be somewhere else, in different company, in a different country.

Finally, Gunnlaugur answered: 'I . . . I don't know. Was it really a man? With a gun?'

And then it was clear that Daníel hadn't been seeing things. A chill spread through his flesh, from head to toe, though a moment ago he wouldn't have believed it was possible to feel any colder.

'It . . . it . . .' Helena stammered, for once losing her cool.

'Yes, a man . . .' Daníel said.

'He, er . . .' Again, Helena tried to speak, but her words trailed off.

'Was he alive?' Ármann asked.

Daníel was about to answer this, then realized he wasn't entirely sure. The man had appeared to be alive, yet he hadn't moved a muscle, just sat there on a chair in the dark corner, staring straight at them. And he had been holding a gun – a shotgun, it had looked like. The sight hadn't only set Daníel's heart pounding fit to burst, it had almost scared the living daylights out of him. A succession of thoughts flashed through his mind. He wasn't naturally afraid of the dark but he couldn't help wondering if he would ever be able to sleep easy again. He felt as if nothing would make him re-enter that hut, and yet, by an irony of fate, if he didn't, he would face certain death outside in the snow. It seemed there was no alternative. Unless . . .

'Can we just go?' he asked, although he already knew the answer to that.

'Go?' It was Gunnlaugur who replied first and Daníel could hear the note of hope in his voice.

'We can't just leave, at least . . .' Ármann sounded uncharacteristically hesitant. He shot a quick glance at Helena, as if seeking approval from her for what he was about to say. 'We'll have to go back in and try to talk to . . . try to find out what's going on. I mean, there are four of us and only one of him.'

'He is alive, isn't he?' Gunnlaugur asked.

'It looked like it,' Daníel said. 'He must be. Come on,

he has to be . . .' Yet he wasn't sure which he would prefer, a dead body or a living man, sitting uncannily still, his eyes wide open in the darkness, waiting for them with a gun . . .

Gunnlaugur

'I'm not going back in there,' Gunnlaugur protested. He hadn't meant to say it aloud but his fear had got the better of him.

'Don't talk rubbish,' Ármann snapped. 'We need to go back inside and deal with the situation. Though you can stay out here and freeze to death, for all I care,' he added grimly.

Ármann started walking back towards the door. Gunnlaugur dithered, his eyes on the others.

Then Helena set off after Ármann and, after a moment's hesitation, Daníel followed.

Gunnlaugur still didn't move. He had been serious: wild horses wouldn't drag him back inside that hut. But as he stood there alone in the snow, his body racked with shivers, it gradually came home to him that he had no choice. They were all in the same predicament and there was no alternative.

Watching the beams of their torches moving about inside, he inched his way closer to the door, reminding himself that he would be shielded by his friends if any-thing went wrong. And he still had his gun. He reached round and took it off his back. Then he lowered his back-pack to the ground, bent down and rummaged among the contents, trying to stop the snowflakes from landing inside, until he found the cartridges. Slowly, hampered by stiff, trembling fingers, he loaded his gun.

After that he felt a bit better.

Frankly, he was astonished that Ármann had charged back in there without taking any precautions of this kind. It was typical of him, he thought sourly. Always the same recklessness, the same over-confidence. Admittedly, that confidence had carried Ármann a long way in life, but Gunnlaugur wouldn't be surprised if it ended up being the death of him one day.

He edged closer to the door, out of the wind, into what should have been their refuge.

Then he slipped off the safety catch on his gun.

Just as a precaution.

Helena

She studied the man who was sitting so still in the corner.

She had never seen him before. He was young, in his mid-twenties at a guess, though it was hard to be sure in the flickering play of torchlight and shadow.

Helena was standing behind Ármann's reassuring bulk. Daníel was behind her and Gunnlaugur presumably still outside. He hadn't followed them in and she still hadn't looked round, too busy keeping her attention fixed on what was happening in front of her.

Ármann directed his torch at the man, who winced perceptibly, closing his eyes against the glare.

'Are you all right, mate? What are you doing here?' Ármann asked. They were hanging back at a wary distance, as far away from the still figure as they could get in the limited space.

The stranger didn't answer, just opened his eyes again and resumed his unnerving stare. He didn't move, or display any threatening behaviour, just watched them in silence, keeping a tight hold of his gun.

'What's your name, mate?' Ármann asked, his tone friendly but firm. 'Are you OK?'

No response.

Startled by a noise behind her, Helena snatched a glance over her shoulder and saw Gunnlaugur step through the door, holding his gun.

'What are you doing with that, Gunnlaugur?' she asked sharply. 'Put it down!'

Gunnlaugur was brought up short for a moment but didn't relax his hold on his weapon. 'I . . . I'm just being careful. We don't want to take any chances.' He sounded more agitated than she would have expected. Then, to her horror, he raised the gun to his shoulder, aiming it at the young man in the corner.

'Gunnlaugur, stop that!' she yelped. 'For Christ's sake, put it down. We're not going to shoot anyone.'

She hadn't spoken to him since last night – had never meant to speak to him again – but she needed to ensure that no one got hit by a stray bullet now. She didn't trust him at all. The truth was that none of them liked him and he must be able to sense the fact. There was a risk that the feeling of being excluded, combined with fear, a confined space and the wild weather, could have potentially lethal results. 'Put the gun down,' she said, slowly and clearly.

When his eyes met hers, she felt a wave of misgiving. Last night, drunk and persistent, he had woken a sense of powerlessness in her that she thought she'd managed to shrug off; a feeling as if she were drowning, as if the oxygen were running out and there was nothing she could do. Whenever she felt like that, her reaction was always the same: that it would be better to sink and drown than struggle on a moment longer.

That's how she had felt for months after Víkingur died, and even now, five years later, she hadn't got over it. That single event that had changed everything. Before, she had been confident, invincible. Death had been a vague concept that happened only to other people. She and Víkingur had been untouchable. She had been in love with him from the first moment to the very last, though they hadn't let her see his body, no matter how much she had begged them.

And now, when she should have been concentrating on the present challenges – on the cold, the blizzard and the armed stranger – all she could see, suddenly, was Víkingur. What she wouldn't have given to have him here beside her now. Then everything would have been all right.

Ármann

'Gunnlaugur, listen to her,' Ármann said, on a note of urgency. He was reluctant to make any move towards Gunnlaugur, unable to judge how close to the edge he was, alarmed by the way his hands were shaking, the crazy glint in his eyes. It came to Ármann that he simply didn't know his erstwhile friend well enough to predict what he'd do.

Yet he had only too clear a memory of Gunnlaugur's reaction when it had really mattered.

Ármann had been stranded in Copenhagen, his leg in plaster, broken in body and spirit. The story he fed Helena was that he'd tripped on the stairs, but the truth was far uglier. He'd fallen foul of a violent thug after getting behind with his payments and refusing to smuggle any more drugs for the man. Ármann had been frightened of ending up in jail, but instead he found himself alone in a foreign hospital. It was then that Helena had stepped in and rescued him. She'd appealed to his friends, collecting enough money to bring him home and pay off his debts.

He'd admitted to her that he had money trouble, while stubbornly clinging to the lie that his fall had been an accident . . .

Helena had saved him, with the help of a few loyal friends. Thanks to them, he'd been able to start a new life back in Iceland, putting the past behind him for good. It had never come back to haunt him. Nowadays he ran a thriving business empire and the sorry tale was known only to the handful of close mates that Helena had turned to for help: Daníel, Gunnlaugur and two or three other people from school. They had all kept quiet about it. And all rallied round to help him – except Gunnlaugur.

Helena had told Ármann about it later. All the others had put their hands in their pockets, although most were hard up themselves. Only Gunnlaugur hadn't replied to any of her messages, and when Helena had eventually called him, he'd refused to take part, saying he didn't have anything to spare and, anyway, people should take responsibility for their own lives.

Take responsibility for their own lives.

The words had continued to echo in Ármann's head for a long time afterwards. He had straightened himself out, driving himself unsparingly, day in, day out, month after month, year after year, never admitting defeat. He had given up all stimulants, except alcohol, and successfully hauled himself out of the abyss. Sometimes he wondered if Gunnlaugur's words might have had a galvanizing effect on him, but mostly he was aware of a deep-seated resentment whenever he recalled them. He knew that one day he would get even with Gunnlaugur for that.

It would have to wait, though, because right now the priority was to dissuade him from waving a weapon around in a tight space where the situation was already volatile enough.

Daníel

Daníel got the impression that Gunnlaugur wasn't going to take any notice of Ármann or Helena. He was still standing in the doorway, his gun trained on the man in the corner, his finger practically on the trigger, and of course none of them had the guts to step into the firing line. Gunnlaugur seemed suddenly unpredictable.

There was a real danger that the situation would end in disaster, yet, ironically, the chief threat came from a member of their own group, not from the armed stranger. Daníel was trying in vain to keep an eye on them both simultaneously, but the darkness didn't help. They had all swapped their head lamps for hand-held torches, but he could shine his only in one direction at a time. Whenever he looked at Gunnlaugur his neck prickled with fear at the thought that, behind him, the stranger might have moved, might even now be springing across the room . . . until he felt compelled to spin round and face him.

But when Daníel directed his torch beam back into the corner, his heart in his mouth, it illuminated the figure sitting motionless in his place, as if nothing could disconcert him and he wasn't remotely alarmed that Gunnlaugur was standing there brandishing a gun and arguing with his friends. Perhaps the eeriest aspect of it all was the stranger's stillness. He was almost like a living corpse, only his open eyes revealing that he was fully conscious and watching them.

Daníel snapped his head back round to Gunnlaugur.

He and Ármann were involved in an argument and things were becoming heated on both sides.

'I have a right to defend myself,' Gunnlaugur shouted, his gun raised to fire.

This was wrong, Daníel thought: at a time like this they needed to stand united, to support each other against the common threat. After all, that's what friends did.

But even as Daníel said this to himself, there was a sick feeling in the pit of his stomach, because he knew, from personal experience, that this wasn't always the case.

'We're all in this together,' he blurted out. 'For Christ's sake, Gunnlaugur, we've got an armed man sitting there, watching us, not saying a word – God knows what he's thinking – and I . . . I'm bloody freezing. I'd give anything to be somewhere else. I don't know what we're supposed to do next. I don't know where or how we're going to get any sleep. All I want is to go to bed but I know that's probably not going to happen any time soon. I can't feel my feet and I feel like shit but . . . But I don't want to get hit by a stray bullet because you're as scared shitless as I am. Can you not just put the gun down . . . ?'

He broke off, exhausted, only to remember, in that

instant, that his attention had been trained on Gunnlaugur the whole time he was talking. Ármann and Helena were staring at him too, as if transfixed. Which meant no one was keeping an eye on the man in the corner. Daníel obeyed the urge to snatch a look, though he hardly dared, convinced that the man would be standing right behind them, breathing down their necks . . .

Gunnlaugur

Gunnlaugur tried to block out the clamour of their voices. He stood his ground, determined that no one was going to take his gun away from him, only vaguely aware that the door was still open, the cold blasting in, freezing his back. He didn't care. The hut was so chilly anyway that there was hardly any warmth to lose.

They had all been shouting at him – Daníel too; having a go at him, though they were supposed to be his friends.

They had all closed ranks against him and now there was that mad-looking bastard in the corner. He was dangerous. Why couldn't the others see it?

Again Gunnlaugur was struck by the realization that he was on his own. And then the suspicion crept into his mind that perhaps it had been one of his so-called friends who had sent him the letters. *Was that possible?*

That first letter had come close to upsetting everything. It had been lying on his desk at work one morning, in an ordinary envelope with his name printed on the front, together with the name of the law firm. Just like any other piece of business correspondence; documents from some colleague or client. Just another letter on the pile in his in-tray; same old routine, every day identical, except this one.

He thought about that letter every day. Lived in dread that the writer would follow through on the threats it had contained. Of course he hoped it would never come to that, but in his weaker moments he felt himself wavering and thinking maybe it would be best to get the whole thing over with.

He hadn't been able to work for a week after receiving the first letter. Even his boss, who wasn't the most perceptive of men, had asked if he was all right – a bit under the weather, maybe? Gunnlaugur had grabbed at the excuse, lying that he thought he might be coming down with flu and taking the rest of the week off sick. But that hadn't been any better. He had sat there alone in his terraced house in Mosfellsbær, with nothing to do but brood on the letter and his job. He would have liked to sleep all day but there was no chance of that, so he had tried instead to distract himself by mindlessly watching TV. Eventually, he had been forced to pull himself together and go back to work, trying to carry on with his life as if no one knew. As if his conscience were clear.

Perhaps this shooting trip, this weekend from hell, was his punishment. His knuckles whitened on the gun.

Then Daníel's voice penetrated his consciousness

again and this time Gunnlaugur made an effort to focus on what he was saying.

'Can you hear me, Gunnlaugur? We're all scared. We're all on the same side. Could you, please, just put the gun down . . . ?'

Helena

For some reason Daníel's words had the desired effect. Gunnlaugur seemed to relax slightly.

It was no surprise to her that he had let himself be talked down. Gunnlaugur had no backbone and would never be capable of standing up to all three of them for long. It wasn't as if he had any other friends, or at least that was the impression Helena got. She kept one eye on him on social media and it was obvious that he didn't exactly have a buzzing social life.

'What . . . then what are we going to do?' Gunnlaugur whispered. He lowered his gun a little and she noticed him fumbling to put the safety catch back on. She hadn't even realized he'd taken it off . . .

She inhaled sharply.

Shit, that could have gone badly.

And it had been Daníel who had managed to talk him down.

He had been genuinely persuasive.

. . . I'm bloody freezing and I'd give anything to be somewhere else . . .

Daníel could come across as so sincere. He'd always found it easy to win people over.

. . . But I don't want to get hit by a stray bullet just because you're as scared shitless as I am . . .

Bravo.

Yet she was never sure when he genuinely meant what he said and when he was acting.

It was one of Daníel's greatest faults – and he had no shortage of those – that he was *too* good an actor, and always had been, long before he went to drama school. She never knew when he was being candid. People were drawn in by his charm but the feelings he bore them in return could be colder than they seemed. Helena had seen a photo of his latest girlfriend and she didn't look a day over nineteen, yet he had obviously managed to charm her too.

Helena followed Daníel on social media as well. He posted a lot of pictures of the new girlfriend, though he had barely mentioned her to them. Instead, he had talked about his success in London, about all the plays he was doing, the opportunities that were opening up. She hadn't seen him act for years, not since before he left for England, but his progress appeared to be unstoppable – assuming he wasn't exaggerating or lying to them . . .

And he was all too capable of that.

Helena could see through him in a way that very few others could. She could see that there was something dark behind the handsome mask. Some quality that people were drawn to, almost in spite of themselves, although deep down they probably knew it was a mistake.

As she knew.

Ármann

'Shut the door, Gunnlaugur,' Ármann said. The cold air had been pouring into the hut all the time they were trying to reason with him but only now did they have a chance to do something about it. Gunnlaugur seemed to have calmed down, temporarily at least. Some of the tension had gone out of his body and he had lowered the gun at last.

Ideally, Ármann would have liked to get the weapon away from him before things went any further, but he decided it might be wisest to solve the problem in stages, one step at a time. Although he didn't trust Gunnlaugur, he reckoned he could handle him. Yet Gunnlaugur was deceptive: he'd shown himself to be surprisingly stubborn. Perhaps the truth was simply that fear affected everyone differently and Gunnlaugur didn't react well to pressure.

Ármann, in contrast, didn't let much knock him off balance. He generally kept his business and his other affairs strictly under control, apart from the time he had made a mess of things in Denmark, but even then he'd had the sense to quit before it was too late, choosing to come home and straighten himself out. At least he could salvage some pride from that.

And now the next matter that required his attention was the man in the corner.

'Come a bit closer,' he said in an undertone, shining his torch round the others' faces and seeing that they were only half listening to him, too distracted by the presence of the stranger. Gunnlaugur obviously couldn't tear his eyes away from the fifth person in the hut and still seemed worryingly jumpy, while Daníel was looking extremely wary. But in spite of their distraction, they obeyed Ármann, shuffling closer into a tight huddle.

'This can't go on – someone will have to talk to him,' Helena said, keeping her voice down.

'Well, it won't be me,' Gunnlaugur whispered immediately. 'No way. You can't make me do it. It's just . . . you'll just have to . . . One of you . . .'

Ármann sighed. Gunnlaugur's reaction didn't come as any surprise. With him it was always the same cowardice, the same selfishness. Had the man ever lifted a finger for anyone else? 'Calm down. No one's asking you to do anything.'

'We're not going to draw lots or toss a coin or anything like that, OK . . . ?'

'No one's even suggested that,' Ármann answered, trying to hang on to his temper. 'So you can just relax.'

'For Christ's sake, no one can relax in a situation like this,' Gunnlaugur snapped back, finally dragging his attention away from the man in the corner and meeting Ármann's eye in the torchlight.

'Something must have happened,' Helena said. 'Perhaps he needs our help. Shall I try?'

Ármann shook his head, lowering his voice to a murmur so there was no risk of it carrying to the stranger. 'Out of the question. It's got to be either me or Daníel. We should be able to take him on if he turns nasty. Obviously we've got to do something because we can't spend the night in a stand-off with an armed man. He looks like he's well equipped and from the way he's hanging on to that gun I'd say he was fully conscious, for what it's worth. Something must have happened . . .'

Ármann turned an enquiring glance on Daníel, moving the torch to illuminate his face. Then, seeing the doubt in his eyes, he saved him the trouble of refusing.

'Fine, I'll do it. You lot keep your eyes open and watch my back.'

'Are you sure?' Daníel whispered, though his relief was blatantly obvious from his tone.

'Of course I'm sure,' Ármann replied, with more of an edge than he had intended. 'Don't worry, I'll take it slowly.'

He scanned their faces, or what could be seen of them in the patches of light and shadow. From their wide eyes and dilated pupils, it was clear that Gunnlaugur and Daníel were seriously spooked.

Ármann turned, his gun still slung over his back, keeping a firm hold on his torch.

It wasn't far to the corner where the man sat, a few metres, no more than six or seven steps. The refuge, which would barely accommodate four people on a good day, would now have to provide room for all five of them. Ármann didn't look over his shoulder but he could almost feel the other three's eyes trained on his back.

Daníel

He watched Ármann.

He could feel his muscles tensing but told himself he mustn't lose his nerve or show any signs of weakness. Above all, he must be careful not to lose his head and freak out. Everything would be fine; that's what he had been telling himself all day, because he had to believe that they would get home safe and sound in the end.

Ármann's movements were slow and ponderous; every time he put his foot down the whole hut seemed to creak, but of course that was fanciful. There was no way of hearing the protesting floorboards over the screeching of the wind outside.

For a second there, Daníel had wondered if he should go against all his instincts and volunteer to talk to the man. To prove himself, perhaps, or at least try to impress his friends with his acting skills. Then he asked himself what for: what was he trying to prove? And what did he have to gain from posing as some kind of hero when they all knew he wasn't one?

And overriding every other consideration was the fear he might die. A numbness spread through his body; he could no longer see clearly in the gloom and was gripped by a sudden feeling of vertigo.

Shit. He had to get a grip on himself.

It would be OK.

It would be OK . . .

Yet he wasn't convinced.

Gunnlaugur

Gunnlaugur had retreated again, until he was standing pressed against the door, ignoring the cold that was still streaming in through the gaps around the frame. Not only did he want to keep well back in case a struggle broke out between Ármann and the man in the corner, he was also concerned to stay as far away from Helena as the cramped proportions of the hut would allow.

Even in the current crisis, last night's debacle was preying on his mind, although he could recall only snatches of what had happened. It was probably a mercy that his memory was so hazy after the booze had taken control. He hoped fervently that Helena wouldn't make any more fuss about it than she already had and that the incident wouldn't be mentioned outside their group. He couldn't afford to have a story like that getting around ... Oh God, please no.

Of course, he hadn't intended any harm, or so he tried to convince himself. He would have stopped even if Ármann hadn't come in. Even if there had just been the two of them there, in the remote hunting lodge, alone together . . .

Like Helena and Daníel, Gunnlaugur was keeping his torch beam trained on Ármann, with the result that the far corner of the hut was brilliantly illuminated while the rest lay in shadow.

'Are you OK?' he heard Ármann asking the man. The stranger had very short hair and looked young and robust, which made his silence and immobility even more uncanny.

Ármann's words were hard to hear over the gusts of wind that kept battering the wooden walls of the hut and screaming over the roof.

There was an oddly charged atmosphere in the room, in spite of the violence of the weather outside, as if this was the calm before the real storm that was about to hit.

Gunnlaugur found himself holding his breath and praying that the man would answer and tell them not to worry, that everything was fine. Then the spell would be broken and they could all have a shot of brandy to help them recover. His thoughts kept returning to the bottle in Helena's backpack. He reckoned he could handle a swig or two. In fact, he couldn't imagine any circumstances in which there would be more justification for a drink than now, to ward off the cold, soothe his nerves and bring him down from his state of extreme agitation. He deserved a shot, but not quite yet; not until Ármann had defused the situation. There would be no way of relaxing properly until he had disarmed the stranger. Gunnlaugur was still holding his own gun and had no intention of surrendering it until the threat had been removed.

The electric silence inside the hut was broken only by Ármann asking again: 'Are you all right?' It was a little harder to hear the words now and Gunnlaugur almost gave in to an impulse to move nearer. But it was clear that the stranger hadn't replied. In fact, he didn't seem to have reacted at all to the question, as if he hadn't heard or understood the words.

Ármann waited a moment, then looked over his shoulder at the others, squinting against the glare of their torches. Gunnlaugur tried and failed to read his expression. Ármann turned back to the man. He seemed to be taking care not to get too close or make any sudden movements that might alarm him.

Then Ármann looked round again and shook his head.

Helena

Ármann came back to join the others, looking uncharacteristically deflated. He put an arm round Helena as if to convey the message to her that everything would work out.

She hoped to God he was right but had begun to realize that there was no guaranteeing it would.

It was Saturday evening. On Saturdays she usually went to the cemetery to visit Víkingur. Hard though it was to explain, she always felt good there, whatever the time of year. Today the graveyard would have been wintry, covered in a layer of snow, perhaps. She always took comfort from walking through the gate, knowing that she was on her way to him, even though they couldn't talk to each other. In summer, when the cemetery was beautiful with all the greenery and flowers, it felt like a refuge from the world, from the cold reality outside. But, oddly enough, she felt more connected to the place – and to Víkingur – in winter, because that was the season in which he had lost his life: cold, exhausted, abandoned and alone.

She would often linger there, talking to him, preferably when no one else was around to overhear. She felt a little foolish communing like this with the dead. Of course, she knew better, and yet she experienced a kind of peace in those moments. She could talk to him about the past and the future, about the things that hadn't gone as well as they might, and the things that were good. Most days had been good.

Yes, in spite of everything, she wished she was in Reykjavík, with him. Although she had been involved in organizing this trip, she had an ominous feeling that it could all end in disaster. Anxiety was getting the better of her, but she told herself she had to be strong. Guns, isolation, fear and uncertainty – they were such an explosive cocktail. And Gunnlaugur was probably the single most volatile factor, the spark that could ignite the powder keg. She would never have believed it, but the events of last night, the effects of drink, insecurity and fear, were all signs that she would have to take seriously.

She looked up at Ármann and shifted a little closer to him. A little further away from Gunnlaugur.

'What did he say?' she asked.

'Not a bloody word,' Ármann answered.

'What?' Gunnlaugur edged towards them.

'He didn't say anything. I don't know what to make of it. He's just sitting there, holding his gun.'

'This is completely crazy,' Daníel said, and Helena heard genuine fear in his voice. 'What are we going to do? Ármann, what the fuck are we going to do?'

'Are you sure he's alive?' Gunnlaugur asked.

Ármann gave him a withering glare and replied harshly: 'For crying out loud, of course he's alive, what does it look like to you?'

Ármann

Ármann noticed that Gunnlaugur was still doubtful. He seemed to withdraw inside himself, his eyes darting back and forth, his expression hard to read. It seemed unbelievable that he could hold down a job as a lawyer. Ármann imagined that in his profession Gunnlaugur must have to stand up for his clients at times, to show some backbone, but he seemed incapable of such a thing. At most he could probably witter on about trivialities, kill a conversation with boredom, but he would never be able to win an argument when there was something real at stake. Perhaps his bosses only entrusted him with the straightforward cases . . .

After a lengthy pause, Gunnlaugur nodded and said: 'Yes, all right, he's alive, obviously, but I just don't understand . . .'

'Shit, none of us understand what's wrong with him. But we've got to resolve the situation somehow. Keep trying to talk to him. I just hope he's . . . Well, that he's . . .'

It was Daníel who finished the sentence for him: 'That he's harmless?'

Ármann nodded.

'There's no way of knowing,' Daníel said. 'This is seriously fucked-up, guys. We –'

'We've got to sort it out. Ármann, *you*'ve got to do something,' Gunnlaugur interrupted. But there was no determination in his voice, only fear and uncertainty. 'Can't we just open that bottle and . . . just sort it out. I'm cold, I need . . .'

'There's no way we're taking decisions under the influence,' Ármann retorted. 'Does it seriously look to you like this is the time and place to sit down and hold a leisurely meeting? We're not at your office now, Gunnlaugur.'

The hut had been designed as an emergency refuge rather than a cosy lodge and offered nothing beyond a basic shelter against the elements. It consisted of a single rectangular room with four windows, two in each of the long walls. The only furniture appeared to be a couple of stools, a small table and bunk beds for four people, which were at the end of the hut closer to the man.

'Has he got any luggage?' Daníel asked.

Ármann shook his head. 'Not that I can see.'

'That's weird. But then nothing about this is normal.'

'No, we're agreed there.' Ármann lowered his voice a little: 'He must have got into trouble of some kind, and normally I'd say we should call for assistance, but since there's no mobile phone signal here, I can't immediately think what to suggest . . .'

'It's dark, there's a blizzard raging outside, we're completely exhausted . . .' Gunnlaugur said, his voice suddenly threadbare.

It might be an idea to let Gunnlaugur have a drink, Ármann thought, in the hope that it would relax him.

'Well, I suppose we could rest, taking it in turns to watch the guy,' he suggested. 'There's enough room for us all to lie down. I'm willing to take the first watch. I reckon I could cope with him if he tried anything.'

'I'm not going to stand guard, not with an armed man in the corner who appears to be off his head,' Gunnlaugur protested. 'There's absolutely no way. Sorry, but it's not going to happen.'

'You're going to do your bit, Gunnlaugur. Don't be so bloody pathetic,' Ármann said harshly, only to regret it as soon as the words were out. Reactions like that did nothing but heighten the tension.

Gunnlaugur winced. 'I mean, I don't know how to . . .'

'We'll solve this together,' Helena said, stepping in. Despite a sometimes prickly temperament, she was generally good at mediating.

'Of course I can try to help,' Gunnlaugur said, backpedalling, 'but I just know I wouldn't be any use if it came to a fight.'

'No, your talents lie elsewhere,' Ármann replied. His anger had cooled, but his words rang false, as he couldn't think of a single talent Gunnlaugur possessed. After a pause, he went on: 'Shall we try it? Getting some rest, I mean, and . . . ?'

He studied their reactions in the light of his torch. Daníel's hesitancy was obvious and Gunnlaugur was transparently terrified. Neither said a word, as if reluctant to be the first to admit aloud that the idea was no good.

It was Helena who spoke up: 'We can't do it, Ármann.' She was calm, almost unnaturally so. 'The plan won't work. That's clear. It's freezing in here and we haven't got any sleeping bags with us. And even if we did, we couldn't use the bunks with that man sitting right beside them. There's no way we'd be able to get any sleep.'

Ármann looked back at Daníel and Gunnlaugur.

Gunnlaugur vacillated but Daníel agreed with Helena: 'She's right, Ármann. It's a crazy idea, I'm afraid. We can't just go to bed as though there was nothing wrong. I'm scared and I don't mind admitting it.'

'Gunnlaugur?' Ármann met his eye and waited.

'I wouldn't be able to get to sleep, even if I tried. That's obvious. And I'm not risking getting into a fight with a possible maniac either. I just don't want – you know – I don't want to die . . .'

'Easy! Calm down. Nobody's going to die. But I take it that my proposal of waiting it out has been rejected. OK, fair enough. We'll . . . we'll just have to work something else out.'

'Is there any chance we could make it to somewhere with a phone signal?' Helena asked. 'Or a radio transmitter? In another hut, for example?'

Ármann paused, before finally conceding: 'I suppose . . . there is a possibility. Should we try that?'

'Is it far to walk?' Helena asked.

'No, not that far,' he replied. 'I'd say about fifteen minutes or so in good conditions – though much longer now, of course. Bugger the Met Office for getting the forecast so wrong.'

'In which direction?'

'South. There's another hut with a radio. I could make a dash for it if someone would come with me for safety's sake. It wouldn't make sense for all of us to risk it, though. I reckon it would take about an hour to get there and back in these conditions, perhaps a bit longer. We could radio for help. Let them know where we are.' Ármann lowered his voice: 'And tell them about the guy in the corner.'

'I'll go,' Helena volunteered. 'You stay and keep an eye on things here. Right now this hut feels more dangerous to me than the storm.'

'Helena, are you sure? If you go, someone will have to go with you. There's no way I'm letting you risk it on your own.' Ármann paused briefly, his eyes seeking out Daníel: 'Would you be prepared to do it, Daníel? To go with Helena and help us out of this mess? We need to call a mountain-rescue team up here, if possible . . .'

'You'd show us the way, wouldn't you?' Daníel asked, doubtfully.

'Yes, as far as I can,' Ármann replied. 'And Helena knows what she's doing.'

'OK, yes, it's a plan. Let's do it,' Daníel said, though he couldn't hide the reluctance in his voice.

'Are you and I supposed to stay here, then?' Gunnlaugur asked Ármann, aghast. 'The two of us, against what might be a dangerous lunatic?'

'Well, he hasn't moved since we arrived. We're armed too and I reckon we could take him if things turned nasty,' Ármann answered. 'Unless you want to go with them?

You're welcome to, Gunnlaugur. I'm perfectly happy to wait here on my own, if you're too scared.'

'No. I'm not going out there again in a hurry. But we're not seriously planning to stay the night here, are we? Taking it in turns to watch and so on?'

'Gunnlaugur, can you just try and man up for once?' Daníel burst out, exasperated. 'If we're going to do this, Helena and I need to make a start. We're already dressed for it. All I need is one nip of brandy and something to eat, then I'll be good to go.'

Ármann could hear from the new note of resolve in Daníel's voice that he wasn't joking. He caught Helena's eye. She took off her backpack, fished out the bottle, uncorked it and took the first swig herself before passing it to Daníel.

Daníel

The brandy burned its way down his throat, sending a warm glow through his body. He immediately took another slug. Much as he dreaded facing the cold and snow again, he had faith in Ármann and Helena. Of course, it would have made more sense for Ármann to take on this challenge himself as he knew the moors and was an experienced outdoorsman, but, faced with the prospect of remaining behind in the hut, Daníel realized he would rather brave the elements. As it was, his nerves were jangling, every muscle was tense and he could hardly wrench his eyes away from the stranger in the corner for more than a few seconds at a time, constantly expecting him to leap up from his seat and launch himself at them or fire his gun in the confined space. The atmosphere was so unreal and oppressive that, in comparison, the uncertainty awaiting them outside didn't seem quite as bad.

What in God's name was the man doing here?

And what had happened to him?

He must have seen or experienced something horrific that had left him in a state of shock.

Daníel didn't even want to pursue that train of thought, for fear that whatever it was could be a threat to them as well.

If they were frightened of this man – which Daníel certainly was – shouldn't they be even more afraid of whatever it was he had seen?

The only sensible reaction was to get out of here as soon as possible. He was just glad he would have Helena's company and wouldn't have to brave the hostile world out there alone. But the alcohol had done nothing to dull his apprehension that there might be something or some-body wandering around out there, and the third slug he took before handing the bottle on to Gunnlaugur prob-ably wouldn't work either. He took a bite of the energy bar which was all he had left in the way of food but felt too sick to have any real appetite.

Gunnlaugur accepted the bottle, his hands visibly shaking, raised it to his lips, then hesitated. For a moment it looked as though he was going to pass the bottle on to Ármann, then he changed his mind and took a large gulp.

It had been a mistake to bring Gunnlaugur along but the blame for that lay entirely with Ármann, and it would serve him right to have to look out for Gunnlaugur as well as himself while Daníel and Helena were away.

'God, that tastes good,' Gunnlaugur said, sounding a little sheepish, and drank again.

At this point Ármann reached for the bottle and took it away from him, firmly replacing the cork.

'Right, OK. Are you two ready?'

'Yes,' Daníel replied, though he wasn't sure it was true. He heaved a deep breath, filling his lungs with the chilly air in the hut, and felt briefly invigorated. 'Shall we get a move on then?' He didn't want to think for too long about the decision that had been more or less taken for him. 'Shall we go?' He sought out Helena's gaze.

She appeared surprisingly unperturbed, but then it had always taken a lot to rattle her. He would have to trust her to get them through this alive.

'Hey,' he said, turning back to Ármann, all the while keeping one eye on the stranger. The man was still sitting utterly still, staring with empty eyes, which in itself was so eerie that it sent a shiver through Daníel's flesh. He felt as if all the warmth had leached from his body. The sensation was similar to when he was coming down with an illness. All this happened in a fraction of a second; he was still standing in the same place, his gaze divided between Ármann and the stranger, the words caught in his throat.

'Daníel, is everything OK?' Ármann asked.

'What?'

'Is everything OK?'

'Yes, er, listen . . .' He had been going to ask a question but could no longer remember what it was.

'OK, good luck. You'll be there and back before you know it . . .'

And then Daníel remembered his question: 'Should we take the guns with us?'

He looked from Ármann to Helena. They were in charge. Gunnlaugur didn't have anything useful to contribute.

'Leave them behind,' Ármann said, as if nothing could be more self-evident. 'You won't have any need of them. It's not as if you're going to shoot any ptarmigan now and the most dangerous creatures you're likely to come across are foxes, which will be more scared of you than you are of them.'

But Daníel's thoughts returned to the man in the corner. *What had he seen or done?*

He had a horrible premonition that there was something out there in the darkness that was more dangerous than a fox, more dangerous than anything his imagination could conjure up . . .

Gunnlaugur

Gunnlaugur was feeling oddly dislocated, as if he wasn't really there but somewhere else entirely.

He no longer felt as miserably cold, just rather numb. Perhaps it was the brandy, perhaps it was his mind playing tricks on him, trying to lull him into a false sense of security. He was aware of the conversation going on around him but just stood there, staring blankly into the shadows. The others didn't seem to notice. For his own sake, he needed to block out the situation for a while by absenting himself in his mind. If he closed his eyes, perhaps the problems would simply disappear.

'What about our backpacks?' he heard Daníel ask. They had been talking about the guns, that was it; about leaving the guns behind.

'No, don't take them either,' Ármann answered. 'They'll only slow you down.'

Gunnlaugur tuned out the voices again. He felt a sudden urge to sit down, as far from the man with the gun as he could get in the small room. He wanted another drink.

Ármann had abstained – ostentatiously, it had appeared to Gunnlaugur. Did he think he was better than them? More dependable? Gunnlaugur curled his lip at the thought. The old druggie Ármann; the man everyone had more or less written off before Helena managed to drag him back from the brink. Perhaps she'd have done better not to have bothered . . .

He leaned back against the door, feeling a little of the tension seeping out of his body, though he was still keeping a firm hold of his gun in one hand. He watched his friends sort out their luggage, filling their pockets with things they might need on their walk.

He would have preferred to dispatch Ármann and Daníel into the storm and be left alone with Helena . . . He wouldn't misbehave, but the thought was enticing; a chance to sit down beside her and try to clear up last night's little misunderstanding . . .

With a jolt, Gunnlaugur remembered the threatening stranger. For a brief moment he had actually succeeded in forgetting where he was.

Suddenly, the contents of the anonymous letters came back to him.

He had to be careful. Of course, he would never do anything wrong but, all the same, he had to watch himself. He mustn't even allow himself to think the sort of thoughts he had been indulging in just now . . .

'You'll be careful, won't you?' Ármann's voice penetrated his consciousness.

'Yes,' he murmured. 'I'll be careful.'

Helena

'No one was talking to you, Gunnlaugur,' Helena snapped. She hadn't meant it to sound that harsh but sometimes she couldn't help herself.

'What?'

'Come on, move. We're leaving.' She gave him a push. He looked completely out of it, as if he had withdrawn into another world. Surely a couple of swigs from the brandy bottle couldn't have had that effect on him?

'What? Oh, right, I'll move.'

She felt a qualm about leaving Ármann behind like this, but believed he had the situation under control.

When she opened the door, the wind hit her with such violence that it was like being attacked by a wild animal. Shocked, she tottered and almost fell over backwards. The snow seemed to be coming down even more thickly than before, if that were possible, sweeping across the landscape in great white sheets. If it had been cold inside the hut, it was brutal out here, but she had to brave it. She couldn't give up now.

'Come on, Daníel. It's now or never.'

He looked dazed and didn't move.

'Come on,' she repeated, and only now did he belatedly react. He stepped past her, bracing himself to keep his balance as he felt the full force of the wind, while she hung back in the doorway, her eyes seeking out Ármann's: 'Which way are we supposed to go?' she asked.

Ármann signalled to her to step outside too, then followed himself.

'Of course, you can't see any landmarks in this weather but that's the general direction.' He held out his arm. 'Just follow the lie of the land. You can't miss it.'

'This is totally insane,' Daníel protested. 'We'll get lost straight away.'

Helena heard him but wasn't sure Ármann had. The screaming of the storm deadened every other sound.

Damn the weather. Damn the forecast.

'Don't be defeatist,' she said. 'We can do it. We'll just keep going in this direction until we stumble across the other hut.'

'Can't you come with us for the first stretch?' Daníel asked, turning to Ármann.

Helena peered at him from under her hood, screwing up her eyes against the stinging pellets of snow. 'I'm confident about this, Daníel.'

'Just for the first bit,' he repeated in a pleading tone, a tremor in his voice.

'What? Oh, OK, I suppose I can do that,' Ármann

said. He zipped his jacket up to the chin, took off his backpack and put it down inside the door of the hut, along with his gun. Then Helena heard him say: 'Hang on, Gunnlaugur. I'll be back in a minute.'

Ármann

Conditions were even more severe than he had antici-
pated, but he'd experienced his fair share of storms and
this wasn't the worst weather he'd ever been caught in.
And Helena was an old hand. She'd accompanied him
on any number of winter trips in the highlands. Nevertheless, he could see that she was alarmed. Daníel,
meanwhile, looked scared to death, as if he expected
this to be his last ever journey . . .

Helena leaned close to Ármann: 'There's no need, you
know,' she said quietly. 'I can handle it.'

'I'll walk with you for the first bit, just to set you on
your way. It's no problem. You can see that Daníel's getting cold feet . . . And nothing must go wrong.'

Daníel couldn't hear them; the wind made sure of that.

Ármann lowered his head and set off, armed with his
torch, then, hearing Daníel call his name, he paused and
looked back.

'What?'

'This is a bad idea!' Daníel shouted.

'It's no big deal, Daníel. Calm down. Come on, follow me. I've been this way countless times before.'

He set off again, striding into the vortex of white flakes whirling in his torch beam.

He heard Daníel calling again but ignored him. He ploughed on doggedly, straight ahead, then took a quick glance over his shoulder to make sure he could still pinpoint the hut, revealed dimly between the curtains of falling snow.

Daníel

'We should turn back!' Daníel shouted again, but neither Helena nor Ármann appeared to hear him.

He had an overpowering premonition that this was a terrible mistake.

That he was heading to his certain death. If they got lost in the highlands in winter, they wouldn't have a chance.

He tried to reassure himself by focusing on how confident the other two were but it was no good. He was following them blindly, in the faint hope that they would lead him to his destination and come to his aid if anything went wrong.

And there was so much that could go wrong.

He could feel himself panicking, although they had hardly walked any distance. How was he supposed to keep going, wading through the ever-deepening snow, screwing up his eyes against the blinding flakes, fending off the numbing cold, all the way to the next hut?

He didn't even have a clear idea of how far they would

have to struggle on, only Ármann's vague reference to a fifteen-minute walk in good weather. He tried to suppress a rising hysteria, but the more he let himself think about the snow and darkness, the more difficult he found it to catch his breath. It was as if the storm were inexorably pressing in on him, stifling him, robbing him of oxygen.

'Ármann,' he called faintly. Then: 'Helena.'

Neither figure looked round.

'Helena!' he called again, a little louder than before. He stopped walking, couldn't go on, not yet.

Finally she responded, turning her head, her face invisible under her hood. Then she tapped Ármann on the shoulder and they both came to a halt.

'Is everything OK, Daníel?' she shouted, starting back towards him.

He was about to say yes but paused. What else could he say? That, unlike them, he wasn't cut out for this. He couldn't cope with the weather. Like a wimp, he wanted to give up. The idea of saying it filled him with shame.

He gasped for breath, flooding his lungs with icy air, then closed his eyes for a moment while the oxygen flowed through his body. He was definitely feeling a bit better. He was tired, that's what was wrong. For an instant he was seized by the urge to lie down in the snow and rest, just for a little while.

Gunnlaugur

It took a minute or two for it to sink in that he'd been left alone in an isolated hut in the highlands with an armed stranger, a man who sat unnervingly still in the corner. He would have resembled a corpse were it not for those unblinking eyes that seemed so alien and sinister. It felt as if he were watching Gunnlaugur – boring his gaze into him – from some other world, some place of darkness . . .

Gunnlaugur recoiled, stumbling into the far corner like a fleeing animal, still clutching his gun. With trembling fingers, he released the safety catch again.

He wasn't going to make any mistakes. Whatever else happened, he was not going to be the victim here . . . Then he settled himself with his torch trapped in the crook of his arm, its beam trained on the man, who didn't move beyond narrowing his eyelids to slits, though Gunnlaugur had the feeling he was still watching him from under them.

Gunnlaugur felt as if his fear must be almost palpable and felt sure that the other man was just waiting his chance, now that it was only the two of them left. It would be a battle of life and death.

Gunnlaugur tried to work out how far apart they were.

A few metres; a few steps; a few seconds. Really only a few brief seconds at best – or worst – if the stranger did decide to jump him . . .

And what if the man raised his gun?

Gunnlaugur didn't even want to let his mind go there. What would he do? Would he have the guts to fire first? He had no way of telling. But what he did know was that he didn't want to die.

Then he remembered the bottle.

Ármann had stuck in the cork and put it down on the floor. It must be here, within reach.

He snatched a glance around, keeping the torch trained on the man so he could catch his every move. But he couldn't see the bottle in the shadows.

Gunnlaugur took a deep breath. He could almost taste the spirits on his tongue. The cold was creeping into his bones again and he was sure a quick swig would warm him up. Of course, he knew better but the danger presented by the man in the corner seemed to retreat before the power of his need, as if nothing mattered beyond having that one little drink. He would have to take a risk and use the light to search for the bottle . . .

Yes, Ármann had left it behind on the floor. Gunnlaugur was sure of it.

Another wave of dread swept over him, stronger than before. Gunnlaugur eyed the still figure in the corner. He was plotting something; he must be.

In his panic, Gunnlaugur had the feeling that the next few seconds or minutes were going to turn into a game of cat and mouse, which he had no intention of losing. But his overriding need now was for a little Dutch courage . . .

The thought of alcohol sent his thoughts ricocheting back without warning to the anonymous letters and the party where he'd met that nice girl. She'd been at university too but studying medicine rather than law. It was the events of that evening that had prompted him to give up drinking. Admittedly, he'd fallen off the wagon again several months later, but the sober intervals had grown longer and longer, until the most recent, which he had just broken, had lasted for two whole years. He had messed up. But everything had to end sometime and there was no point shedding any tears over it now. And no reason to quit again quite yet . . .

Yes, he'd been instantly attracted to the girl and struck up a conversation with her, telling her about his abortive medical studies. Although she'd been perfectly polite and friendly, he had suspected that his interest wasn't reciprocated. Nevertheless, they had continued chatting until late into the night. Because, the thing was, he *could* actually be interesting when he put his mind to it, or at least that's what he told himself. During the course of the evening, they had both downed far too many drinks and . . .

He'd had good reason for his decision to give up booze after that night.

And he had good reason now for craving a bit of Dutch courage.

The man hadn't moved.

Gunnlaugur went for it. He lowered his torch beam to the floor and as he swept it around in search of the bottle, time seemed to pass with agonizing slowness. It wasn't there, he told himself in despair; they must have taken it with them . . .

Then he spotted the little darling, just out of reach. He couldn't quite stretch out his arm to take it; he'd have to bend down a bit, shift along, a step or two, and . . .

Yes, he'd got it.

The bottle was in safe hands.

He had no idea how long it had taken him, perhaps only two or three seconds, maybe more. But it would certainly have given the man enough time to reach his corner, raise his weapon and aim it straight at Gunnlaugur.

Gunnlaugur closed his eyes, too frightened to look up.

Helena

Death was never far away in weather like this, as Helena had learned from bitter experience.

Summer or winter, nature could be magnificent, but under the dazzling surface it was lethal. Going astray in the highlands was no different from getting lost in a desert; the cold as dangerous as the heat. Even beautiful summer days could be deadly in the Icelandic wilderness, where there was no shelter to be had if the weather suddenly turned, and no way of keeping out the cold.

Helena couldn't think of anything more horrible than that merciless cold.

She had read up on hypothermia, without wanting or meaning to, unable to stop herself. About how the body gradually lost heat, its temperature falling, the organs beginning to fail, one after another: heart, kidneys, liver . . . until finally there was nothing but oblivion.

Several months after Víkingur died, she had looked it up to see if it was a painful death. The doctors had assured her it wasn't but she hadn't believed them. It had been a huge relief to learn that the internet agreed with the doctors.

Yet no matter how often she read it, how often she recalled the doctors' words, deep down she was convinced that Víkingur had suffered unbearable torments throughout his ordeal, right up until he drew his very last breath in the cold.

Ármann

The moment Ármann opened the door his instincts kicked in, warning him that something was wrong. His heart began to beat faster and he snatched a quick glance around, wary, scared even, though he would never have admitted it.

He had switched off his torch and put it in his pocket, having taken care not to go too far from the hut.

The far corner where the man had been and was hopefully still sitting was in total darkness, but in the opposite corner, near the door, he was aware of a movement and a pool of light illuminating the floor. He pulled out his torch and switched it on.

The beam caught Gunnlaugur in the act of bending down to reach for something. What the hell was he up to?

After a second's delay, Gunnlaugur glanced up, as if he had only just noticed that Ármann had returned.

'Is everything OK?' Ármann asked sharply.

He checked the other end of the hut. The man was still

there in the corner. The screaming of the wind, the fraught atmosphere, they were unchanged.

Then it dawned on him that Gunnlaugur must have been reaching for the brandy bottle.

'Is everything OK?' Ármann repeated.

'What, oh, yes, or . . .' Confused, Gunnlaugur swung his torch back and forth between the man in the corner and Ármann, and it seemed to take him several seconds to gather his wits. 'Yes, I think so. You were such a long time.'

Ármann couldn't have been away for more than a few minutes but no doubt time had crawled past with agonizing slowness for Gunnlaugur, left behind in a tense stand-off with the stranger. The fear was radiating off him and he still had his gun clamped under his arm. Then, without warning, Gunnlaugur slid down the wall until he was sitting on the floor, the bottle in his other hand.

'Just relax, Gunnlaugur. It's going to be fine. You can have a bit of a rest, if you like. I'm not tired. There's nothing to worry about.'

'I'm not going to have a rest, not right now. I'm not letting my guard down. You can't order me around.' Gunnlaugur put down his weapon briefly in order to uncork the bottle and swig from the neck, or rather tip back his head and pour the spirit down his throat.

Ármann felt a stirring of alarm. He toyed with the idea of jumping Gunnlaugur and grabbing the gun, unhappy with the idea of him being armed and drunk. Let him hang on to the bottle, but the gun was another matter.

Ármann didn't risk it, though. Not at this stage. He

would have to reduce the tension thrumming in the air first, then await his chance. Besides, he needed a rest himself. He had been lying when he told Gunnlaugur he wasn't tired. In reality, he was worn out.

He lowered himself to sit on the floor in his turn, leaning back against the wall, careful not to get too close to Gunnlaugur. Then he reached into his backpack and, pulling out a bar of chocolate, offered it to Gunnlaugur in a gesture of friendship. With any luck this would help calm the atmosphere. Ármann didn't like the way Gunnlaugur was drinking on an empty stomach but they'd eaten their packed lunches hours ago and the chocolate was all he had left.

Gunnlaugur took the proffered bar in silence and broke off an over-generous helping for himself.

'I'm just going to catch my breath,' Ármann said. 'We don't need to take any decisions straight away, OK?'

'Sure, do what you like. I have no intention of going to sleep. But don't expect me to watch your back. It's every man for himself now, and you'll just have to accept it, I'm afraid.'

'We're not in any immediate danger, mate. Surely, you can see that?' Ármann raised his voice slightly. 'We're two against one.'

'What if he threatens us with the gun?' Gunnlaugur asked in an undertone, as if afraid the stranger would hear. Then suddenly: 'We could throw him out, couldn't we? Why don't we do that?'

'Are you out of your mind? We're not throwing him outside to die of exposure.'

Gunnlaugur was silent for a moment, then whispered: 'Then let's tie him up. OK?'

'Tie him up? Why? Do you really think that would achieve anything?'

'He's freaking me out. And I want . . .' Silence again. 'I just want a rest.'

Ármann was momentarily at a loss. He was finding it hard to read Gunnlaugur's reactions, beyond the fact that he seemed worryingly jittery.

'OK,' he said eventually.

'OK, what?'

'OK, you can tie him up. Go ahead. Do as you like. Got a rope, have you? Just how did you envisage doing it? Tie him to . . . well, to what? You don't think he'll resist? Oh, and another thing – how were you planning to wrestle his gun off him?'

Gunnlaugur was silent.

And Ármann breathed a little easier.

Daníel

He followed Helena, staying as close to her as possible. On no account must he lose sight of her.

Fifteen minutes' walk, Ármann had said. In ideal conditions. Perhaps an hour there and back in this storm. They must have been walking for ten minutes already but it was difficult to keep track. Daníel's sense of time was confused; reality seemed increasingly remote. He didn't wear a watch and his phone was buried deep in a pocket of his down jacket. He would just have to have faith in Helena.

He picked up his pace a little, catching up with her sufficiently to grab her shoulder.

She stopped and turned. 'All right?'

He nodded, panting. 'Any idea how much further it is?'

'Yes. Another ten minutes, at a rough estimate. We've made faster progress than I was expecting. And the snow's not as deep as I was afraid it might be. I reckon the weather might be improving a bit too.'

Improving? Daníel peered around through the snow

that had collected on his lashes. The blizzard seemed to form a wall of white on every side, making the view identical in every direction. Visibility was reduced to a few metres at best.

'OK. Look, I just don't have a good feeling about this,' Daníel said in a rush. 'It's making me almost claustrophobic.' He hadn't meant to reveal his weakness to her, but it was true. In fact, the feeling was worse than claustrophobia, it was almost like being buried alive.

Helena turned away as if to start walking again but didn't move.

Then she stared back at Daníel, looking as if she had seen a ghost; her expression abruptly changed, her gaze clouded.

Had Helena lost her nerve? That would be the worst thing that could happen in the circumstances.

Daníel took a step backwards, peering around again. There was nothing to see but whiteness, and suddenly, to his horror, he realized he was no longer sure which direction they had come from.

'Helena?'

'Sorry. Let's keep going,' she said, yet she seemed undecided. After a pause, she added: 'Sorry. I was just thinking about Víkingur.'

'Víkingur?'

'Yes, about how he must have felt when he was dying . . .'

Daníel shuddered. He didn't know what to say and wanted to beg her to change the subject, but of course he couldn't do that. So he said nothing, just pretended the storm had swallowed her words.

They had been inseparable, Víkingur and Helena. Nothing had ever come between them. The perfect pair; glamorous, intelligent . . .

'Let's go on,' she said, after a brief, awkward silence.

Daníel set off reluctantly in her wake. All his instincts were screaming at him to turn back. They were probably still closer to the hut they had left than the one they were making for. Part of him would have liked to abandon Helena and leave her to cope on her own, but right now she was the only thing keeping him alive; without her he would be totally helpless.

He lowered his head against the wind and snow, catching his breath. One step at a time and he would make it to their goal. All he had to do was follow doggedly in Helena's footsteps.

He raised his head again, the moment of panic over, but just as he did so, Helena seemed to lose her footing. She tripped and fell flat on her face in the snow, emitting a scream of pain. No one but him could have heard her cry, but it was so piercing and eerie that he had never heard anything like it. Instead of muffling it, the snow seemed to magnify the sound and the wind screamed in sympathy.

Daníel froze and stood there stiff with fright, gaping at her as if it was someone else's job to come to her aid and he were no more than an onlooker. Then it dawned on him that he was the only one who could help.

Gunnlaugur

Gunnlaugur had perked up a bit after the chocolate and brandy. The alcohol had taken the edge off his anxiety, though he still couldn't properly relax. He knew better. The danger hadn't gone away and he was afraid of succumbing to his fatigue. But the drowsiness stealing over him was cunning and he was so tired from the hours slogging across the moors, then battling the wind-driven snow.

It didn't help to have Ármann sitting just over there, still and silent, as if he had given up the fight. It seemed it really was a case of every man for himself.

Gunnlaugur suspected that if it came to a struggle, Ármann wouldn't even try to defend him. The two of them had never really hit it off and their present predicament had exposed their differences more starkly than ever. There was no room here for pretence, no time for small talk, to smooth things over.

He was still nursing his gun, though he wasn't gripping it as tightly as before, and the bottle was reassuringly close to hand. He could do with another drink to ward off the icy draught that was streaming under the door and cutting through his clothes to the bone. The hut was barely insulated at all and sitting still like this didn't help. He could no longer feel his toes. His stomach rumbled – the chocolate had done little to satisfy his hunger – and his mouth was dry but his water bottle was empty and there was no way he was risking a trip outside to try to quench his thirst with snow. Who knew what might happen in his absence?

He picked up the brandy bottle again, raised it to his lips and drank, then placed it on the floor.

Drowsiness crept up on him, like a wild beast stalking him in the silence, and struggle as he might, he had no means of defending himself against its wiles.

Helena

'What happened?' she heard Daniel shouting. 'Helena, are you all right?'

She turned warily onto her side, sensing how quickly the snow was stealing the warmth from her body.

'I . . . I . . .' She paused. 'I tripped.'

'Let me help you up . . .' He held out his hand.

'I think – ow! – I think I've sprained my ankle.'

Even through the snow and darkness she thought she saw Daniel blench as her words reached him.

'Sprained your ankle? You can't have.'

She struggled to her knees, then rose cautiously, putting most of her weight on her other leg. 'Yes. Shit, I think I have. I'm not sure, but it's . . . shit, it hurts. It's unbelievably painful.'

'You must be able to make it the rest of the way to the hut?' From the rising note of anxiety in his voice she could tell that now, as ever, he was thinking only of himself.

'I'm trying, Daniel, I'm trying, all right?' she yelled, so loudly that he flinched.

'OK, sorry. Can I help you?'

Moving closer, he held out his hand.

'Thanks,' she said quietly, taking his arm, and hopped forward on one foot.

'Why don't you try putting some weight on it?' he asked urgently.

'OK, I'll try,' she said, only to yelp when she did as he suggested. 'It's . . . it's . . .' She groaned. 'I'm sorry, Daníel, it's no good . . .'

'What do you mean?' he asked, unable to disguise the panic in his voice.

'I don't know if I can make it all the way . . . I . . .'

'You have to, Helena, you . . .'

'All right! Calm down, OK?'

He nodded but she could see that he was frantic.

'I don't know how far I can get, hopping on one foot like this. Maybe I could wait here for you, Daníel. I reckon the storm's dying down a bit . . .'

'What? Then what am I supposed to do?'

'Go on and find the hut. Use the radio to call for help. Then you'll have to come back for me . . .'

'You could die, Helena.' He hesitated, then said: 'And I might not be able to find you again.'

'You'll have to, Daníel. Or I can try to get back to the others on my own and you can wait in the other hut for help to arrive . . .'

He interrupted: 'No way. You're coming with me . . .'

'It's further in that direction – not as far to get back. Come on, don't be stupid,' she said harshly. 'You're going to have to shape up.'

'OK, yes, I . . .'

'It'll be fine, I promise. You'll save us, Daniel. Remember that. We're all relying on you.'

He nodded and set off slowly, doubtfully. But after a couple of steps he paused and looked round.

'Are you absolutely sure?' he asked.

'I trust you, Daniel.'

She watched as he headed off into the unknown, the veils of snow closing behind him.

Ármann

A strange peace had descended in the primitive hut.

Gunnlaugur hadn't moved from his spot. Ármann could see only his dim outline in the shadows, now that he no longer had his torch trained on him, but as far as he could tell Gunnlaugur had fallen asleep.

Helena and Daníel had been gone quite a while.

Ármann finally felt able to relax a little. As often happened when he let himself switch off, his mind ranged back to his years in Copenhagen, when his life had so nearly come to a premature end . . .

There had been times when he would have welcomed the idea; when his debts were piling up and he could no longer fund his addiction. Worst of all had been his fear of the men who threatened him with dire punishments if he didn't pay up, when he had lived in dread of the pain and danger that could be lurking around every corner. In the main, though, he had got off lightly, apart from the occasional beating. That was until the fateful evening when he had been ambushed by two men, one of them a dealer to whom he owed a substantial sum of money. They had hurled him downstairs with such force that he had been pretty sure his number was up. It had been an extremely close shave, but by pure luck he had escaped – if you could call it that – with no more than a badly broken leg. That was the point at which Helena had flown out to Denmark and rescued him, and he would never forget it.

Ármann was well aware that he hadn't been entirely blameless. He had beaten people up during his years as an addict, and, although he had never killed anyone, he knew deep down that he was capable of it. Naturally, he had abstained from that sort of behaviour ever since he had gone straight and set up his company. Nowadays, he never talked about the past, even to Helena, and banned anyone else from referring to it, deliberately surrounding himself with a new circle of friends, with the exception of Gunnlaugur and Daníel. They were aware of what had happened in Copenhagen, or at least an edited version of the story.

Ármann could be ruthless. It had always been part of his character, though he tried to keep it hidden. He reckoned it must be in his genes. He also held firmly to the belief that ruthlessness equalled success. And there was no question that he had been successful in recent years.

But the memory of the men who had wanted to maim him still kept him awake at night. The thugs who had thrown him downstairs and the others who had at various times either threatened him or beaten him up. All their faces seemed to merge into one: an inscrutable stranger, aged between twenty and thirty, heavily built and strapped with muscle.

More often than not it was men in this age group, powerfully built types, that he employed to work for him, either in his travel company or in the construction business, an area he was now branching out into. Whenever he met a new employee who reminded him of his Copenhagen days, he felt a frisson of the old fear run through him, just for a split second, because of course he knew it was his imagination playing tricks on him. The sensation was unsettling, nonetheless. An unwelcome reminder of his vulnerability.

Ármann liked to be in control of his surroundings, to be the one running the show. It was why he hadn't taken a single drop of brandy since they entered the hut. And why he was sitting perfectly still now in the shadowy room, watching. It didn't once cross his mind to close his eyes.

Gunnlaugur

'Medicine, you said?'

He could remember every word of his conversation with the girl, could still picture her: the long blonde hair, the guarded smile.

'Yes, and you?'

'Law.'

He had offered her a drink. First one, then another, and so on late into the night. She had been so pretty, so easy to talk to, right up until the end, though her gaze had grown increasingly glazed as the evening wore on. At some point everyone else had left the room where they were chatting, her friends were somewhere else in the house, and he'd decided to go for it, only to find her resisting him, saying something he couldn't quite understand, or didn't want to understand. But somehow he had convinced himself that it was meant to happen, that she wasn't really unwilling. His memory was a bit of a blur, but when he woke up the next morning with a crippling hangover he knew he had crossed a line, and just hoped that she had experienced things differently or, better still, didn't remember anything at all. It wasn't until two years later that he had received the first letter. It was presumably far too late for her to prove anything, but she – or perhaps a friend of hers – had clearly decided that he shouldn't be allowed to forget it. According to the letter, the anonymous sender was in possession of information that could destroy his life. The letters were only a warning, no demands had been made as yet, but they'd had the desired effect. Gunnlaugur's sleep had become fitful and every morning when he awoke he wondered if today would be the day when the girl, or whoever was behind the threats, sent the same kind of letter to his boss.

He had never run into her again after that night but lived in fear of an encounter. As far as was possible, he watched her from a distance, via social media, so he knew which hospital she worked at and who she associated with. They hardly had any acquaintances in common, but one day, in a country as small as Iceland, it was almost inevitable that their paths would cross . . .

She was always the same when she appeared in his nightmares: innocent, smiling, pretty. Her eyes pleading for mercy.

Gunnlaugur woke with a jerk.

He was enveloped in darkness and for a moment or two he couldn't remember where he was. Then it came back to him, like a blow. He had nodded off. Shit. Fumbling for the torch in his lap, he switched it on and flashed it around the room.

To his relief, the man was still in his corner, but now he was watching Gunnlaugur, almost as if he knew . . .

Ármann was sitting by the door, wide awake. He didn't speak, just nodded when he saw that Gunnlaugur was awake too.

The atmosphere was so tense that Gunnlaugur wished he'd gone on sleeping. He was still dead tired and his nightmare about the girl was no worse than the reality staring him in the face.

But Ármann showed no signs of dropping off and everything was quiet. It must be safe to let his eyelids close again, Gunnlaugur thought, just for a minute, while he was gathering his strength. Somehow the darkness in his dreams hadn't seemed as bad as the darkness in the hut.

He only meant to allow himself a brief nap.

It would be all right. Nothing would happen.

Helena

She had never seriously doubted her ability to find her way back, but it was still a huge relief when she finally saw the dim outline of the hut looming through the darkness. The storm had lost some of its fury, which helped, and she'd always had a good sense of direction. She had done her best to memorize the lie of the land, though it was hard with so few landmarks visible through the snow. A cairn here, a stream there. One thing was certain: she had absolutely no intention of dying tonight.

She took hold of the door handle and for one horrible moment she thought it was locked. Her stomach lurched and she felt weak with dread, but next minute the door gave way slightly, though there still seemed to be some hindrance blocking it inside. Again, she felt a flash of panic that there might have been a disaster, but then she managed to push the door far enough open to step inside, and walked almost straight into Ármann.

She flung her arms around him. Of course everything was all right. Of course Ármann had the situation under control, as always. He had his faults but, if anything, they had only made him stronger as the years went by.

'Is everything OK?' he asked, sounding worried.

She nodded. It was almost pitch black inside; Ármann's torch was on the floor, illuminating only the lower part of the wall.

'Are they . . . ?' she began, but didn't finish her question as a blinding light suddenly caught her full in the face.

'Helena?' It was Gunnlaugur. 'Are you back?'

'I . . . er, I had a bit of an accident on the way.'

'What? What happened?' Ármann asked, his voice full of concern. 'Did you hurt yourself? Where's Daníel?'

'I think I've sprained my ankle,' she said in a low voice, and limped the rest of the way into the hut so that she could close the door behind her, though it was so chilly inside that it made little appreciable difference.

'Where the hell's Daníel? Did you manage to radio for help?'

Helena hesitated a moment, then heaved a deep breath. 'He went on.'

'Alone?' Gunnlaugur asked incredulously.

'Yes. It was pretty brave of him,' Helena said. 'I wasn't expecting that. Don't worry, he'll get help.'

'Good old Daníel. I knew we could rely on him,' Ármann said. 'Now all we have to do is wait.' He continued on a softer note: 'Are you sure you're OK, Helena? Do you want us to take a look at your ankle? There's a first-aid kit in my pack.'

Gunnlaugur interrupted before Helena could answer: 'How long are we supposed to wait? Do any of us really trust Daníel to do this? Because – I have to be frank with you – I don't.'

Helena smiled wryly. All it took was a bit of pressure or a crisis of some sort to bring out the worst in people and expose them for what they were. Daníel had always looked after Gunnlaugur but now, when the chips were down, Gunnlaugur was quick to turn his back on his old friend. While it didn't surprise her, she would at least have expected Gunnlaugur to do a better job of disguising his feelings.

'We'll wait as long as it takes,' Ármann said. 'But hopefully that won't be too long.' He turned back to Helena: 'What do you think, should we take a look at your foot?'

She shook her head. 'No, it's not as bad as I thought at first. I can't put my full weight on it but I doubt it's anything serious, thank God. Don't worry about me. I'll go to the doctor when I get back to town. But for now all we need to do is sit tight and wait.'

Ármann

Ármann had let Helena have the first rest while he kept
watch. It was becoming increasingly difficult to keep his
eyes open as the night wore on but over the years he had
trained himself to stay awake as long as necessary. No
doubt this could be traced to his life in Copenhagen,
when his nights had been spent either doing drugs or too
frightened to sleep, or a combination of both. What he
wouldn't have given right now, he thought, for a good,
strong coffee.

The three of them had discussed how best to organize things during the night and once again Gunnlaugur
had refused to do his bit, obstinately insisting that he
wasn't going to stand guard over the stranger. He was
totally useless, but, on the other hand, as long as he had
hold of that gun he constituted a threat himself. It was
vital to keep an eye on him and try to draw some of the
tension out of the atmosphere. Hang on in there until
daybreak.

The upshot was that Ármann and Helena had decided

to sleep in shifts, as far as possible. Now she appeared to be sound asleep at his side; he could take his turn later.

And Daníel . . .

Ármann wondered how he was coping out there in the snow and where he might be now . . .

Gunnlaugur

It was still dark. Gunnlaugur, who had failed to get back to sleep, had been sitting there with his eyes closed, trying to doze. It was as if his body refused to accept that it was beaten.

The trouble was that Gunnlaugur didn't trust a single person in that hut. As far as he was concerned, staying alert could easily be the difference between life and death.

Of course, it could be paranoia and disorientation brought on by his decision to start drinking again, he was aware of that, but it was better to be careful all the same. He had to be prepared in case something happened. He hugged his gun close to his chest.

Reluctant though he was to trust Ármann or Helena, he had no choice but to put all his faith in them when it came to getting home, because he knew he would never be able to find his way back to the hunting lodge where they had stayed last night. Or to locate the other hut that Daníel should have reached by now – with any luck . . .

But Gunnlaugur knew his old friend too well to be

161

confident of that. Daníel might be physically fit but he had never been the outdoorsy type or good at handling pressure. Which made it ironic that he should have ended up playing the role of saviour for the group.

But with luck, he thought, everything would look better when the light finally returned tomorrow morning.

Gunnlaugur still had his torch on, though he wasn't sure how long the battery would last. He avoided pointing it directly at the stranger in the corner, afraid of provoking him, but he could make out his outline and was poised to leap into action if the man moved so much as a muscle. Gunnlaugur felt he was ready for anything; in fact, he reckoned he would even be prepared to fire his gun, if he felt threatened enough.

Sunday

Helena

A faint grey light was filtering into the hut when Helena surfaced.

She must have been asleep much longer than she'd intended.

Instantly alert, she sat up and peered around.

'Awake?' Ármann asked affectionately.

She rubbed her eyes. 'Have you been up all night?'

'All night and through to morning. I can sleep later.'

'Is everything OK?' she asked hesitantly. As her eyes adjusted, she made out Gunnlaugur and the man in the corner, still in his place. Both appeared to be asleep.

'Everything's fine,' Ármann reassured her.

'Has Daníel . . . ?'

'He's not here. I haven't heard anything.'

Helena was silent.

She got warily to her feet, still a little groggy and stiff, waiting for her circulation to get going again. Her hands and feet were numb with the cold.

'It'll be fine,' Ármann said again.

She smiled at him.

Then she checked on the others. Neither Gunnlaugur nor the stranger had stirred.

She couldn't wait to get home, back to her daily routine, to work. It would be Víkingur's birthday soon. She celebrated it every year by going out to dinner alone, always to the same place, their favourite restaurant. Every year she was relieved to find that it hadn't closed down, as she couldn't bear the thought of having to choose a new place or change any detail of her ritual. It was where they always used to celebrate their birthdays and where so many good memories had been born. Víkingur had been so handsome; tall, warm and loving, at times so determined and ambitious, at others so thin-skinned and insecure. It had been these contrasts that made him unique, and Helena knew that without him she would never be the same again. There would always be something missing. She could have borne to lose him to another woman's arms. That would have been painful, agonizingly so, but at least he would have been happy.

Instead he had died, alone.

She hadn't even had a chance to say goodbye.

It made her unbearably angry every time she thought about it.

A pointless, horrific way to die.

Perhaps he had simply been too beautiful and sensitive to survive in a hard world. If it hadn't been then, perhaps it would have happened later. That was what she tried to tell herself when she was at rock bottom, but she knew it was fanciful; an attempt to soften the darkness with a little light. Because the darkness inside her was unrelenting, though she hid it well.

She managed to smile through her tears, pretending to be somebody else, concealing her true self. It was the only way she could carry on.

She had decided from the very first not to give up.

He wouldn't have wanted that.

A shooting trip like this would have been wonderful if Víkingur had been there, even if they'd been caught in a blizzard. She would have taken care of him, as she should have done back then.

If and *should have* . . .

Hearing a noise, she snapped her head round.

The man was stirring.

Ármann

At last the end was in sight.

It was morning. According to the ridiculously expensive watch on his wrist – a present to himself to celebrate a record year – the new day was quite advanced, though the light kept one waiting in November. The windows were plastered with snow and he couldn't see out but Ármann could hear that the wind had lost much of its force. They shouldn't have any trouble making it back to the lodge once it was properly light.

Helena was awake and seemed in fairly good spirits, considering.

Gunnlaugur was still fast asleep, not that Ármann gave a damn what sort of state he was in. All that mattered was to get him safely back to town with them. After that, they would cut all ties with him, as they should have done long ago.

'He's waking up, Ármann,' Helena whispered suddenly.

'What?' Ármann looked first at her, then automatically at Gunnlaugur.

'No, not Gunnlaugur. Him . . .' She pointed into the far corner.

Ármann turned back to her and nodded. 'OK, I'll deal with it.'

He rose cautiously to his feet. Leaving the gun behind but taking the torch, though the darkness inside the hut was no longer as impenetrable as it had been during the night, he moved slowly and calmly towards the man. As he did so, he cast the occasional glance at Gunnlaugur, who appeared to be sleeping peacefully. That was strange in the circumstances, but, then again, perhaps not so strange when you considered the inroads he'd made into the bottle.

At last the end was in sight, he thought again.

It had been a gruelling day and a bizarre night, to say the least.

The man had gone to sleep in his corner, sitting upright, propped against the wall. Amazing how well people could adapt, Ármann thought. He himself had resolved to stay awake all night and had managed to do so, in spite of everything, successfully fighting off his fatigue. Of course, his gnawing hunger had helped. But he was quite proud of himself. He could sense that the tiredness was still lurking under the surface, though, just waiting to ambush him, but he would have to hold it off: today he was going to need his wits about him.

He had reached the man now and was standing very close to him. He bent down, closer still.

Gunnlaugur

Something had disturbed him.

Perhaps it was the sound of one of the others moving about or perhaps he had been warned by some sixth sense that something was wrong.

He occasionally gave in to the impulse to believe in unexplained forces, though he never mentioned this to anyone. They wouldn't understand, but then they weren't to know that his grandfather had been a well-known psychic in his day. Gunnlaugur sometimes wondered if he had inherited the gift, if only to a limited extent. Perhaps he was more receptive than most. That could be one reason why he found it so difficult to make close friends or hold on to girlfriends ... He felt oddly out of step with other people. He hadn't managed to get rich either, in spite of a genuine desire to make money. When he saved up to buy shares, their value invariably plummeted. A colleague of his at the law firm had invested in property, getting in on the game early before house prices had shot up to such extortionate levels, and now owned several flats. He was raking it in, managing his properties in the evenings and working as a lawyer by day. But there was no point in Gunnlaugur comparing himself to people like that.

Life felt like a constant uphill struggle and at times Gunnlaugur had to remind himself to be grateful for the quality of life he did enjoy. Too often his negativity got the better of him.

He had been asleep, that was clear. And it would take him a while to adjust to the darkness again. Perhaps it was morning, perhaps not; it was impossible to tell, but it couldn't be that late as it still wasn't light.

He felt utterly exhausted and gradually became aware of the throbbing in his head. It came back to him that he had put away rather a lot of the brandy last night and was probably still a little the worse for wear.

For a moment, as he surfaced, he had forgotten where he was and what was going on, as sometimes happened when he woke up in an unfamiliar environment. The feeling hadn't lasted long this time and yet it had been all the more comforting, as if a heavy burden had briefly been lifted from his shoulders.

But now the grinding cold and hunger made their presence known again.

He could hear nothing but the whining of the wind.

Were the others still here?

All of a sudden he was hit by the fear that he was alone in this wretched hovel. Alone, or – even worse – alone with the sinister stranger. Panic-stricken, he sat up stiffly, with the idea of shifting closer to the wall, then realized that he was already pressed up against it and couldn't go any further.

'Daníel?' he croaked, keeping his voice down but hoping it would carry far enough for his friend to hear. 'Daníel?'

His oldest friend, the only member of the group he could trust. Surely Daníel was here with them?

His eyes were beginning to adapt to the gloom and he groped around him clumsily in his gloves, trying to find his torch or phone, something that could shed light on the situation. Instead of either, he felt a hard shape that he identified, after a moment's confused fumbling, as the bottle – but he left it there and felt for his gun instead, closing his grip on the weapon. It was just as well to be prepared.

'Daníel?' he whispered again.

A hand was laid on his shoulder, causing him to jump out of his skin. His fingers tightened convulsively on the gun.

'It's only me – Helena.' Her voice was soft and steady, and his tense muscles relaxed a little.

'Oh, OK.'

'Daníel's not here, remember? I –' She broke off, then went on: 'I'm worried about him. He went out with me yesterday evening to find the other hut, remember? But we haven't heard anything from him since.'

In a rush, the whole thing came back to Gunnlaugur, through his hangover and bleariness: Daníel and Helena had both gone out there but only one of them had come back. He felt an odd foreboding that Daníel was dead.

Perhaps it was the note in Helena's voice, hinting that she wasn't expecting Daníel to make it back alive. Gunnlaugur strained his ears, listening to the desolate moaning of the wind, sure that he himself would never have been able to find the way if he had been left to fend for himself out there. He would almost certainly have given up and let himself die. He was no hero and never had been.

'What about Ármann?'

'Ármann's here with us. Don't worry, this will be over soon. It's a new day, though you wouldn't know it with the snow covering the windows like this.'

Gunnlaugur felt a wave of relief. He believed Helena. He didn't have the energy or will to do anything else. There was no room in his head now for any thought apart from the need to go home.

Helena

She removed her hand from Gunnlaugur's shoulder.

Touching him had sent a shudder through her flesh, but all that mattered now was keeping him calm. He was a total loose cannon, as they had seen, and she was uneasily aware of how much he had drunk. There was astonishingly little brandy left in the bottle.

She mustn't forget for one minute that he was holding a firearm and had a jittery trigger finger. Swallowing her loathing, she made a great effort to speak gently to him.

Soon they would be free of this nightmare and she would be able to relax.

'Shouldn't we be looking for Daníel?' she heard Gunnlaugur ask, with a blast of stale brandy fumes.

'We daren't risk it,' she said. 'The snow's bound to have drifted during the night and it would be dangerous for us to waste precious time searching for him now. Our priority is to get ourselves back to safety. As soon as we have a phone signal, we can alert the mountain-rescue teams. It'll be daylight soon and Ármann and I are sure the gale is blowing itself out. Once it does, we'll head off together, looking out for each other.'

'But what about . . . ?' Gunnlaugur didn't finish the sentence but it was obvious he was referring to the stranger.

'Ármann will deal with him. We can trust him to sort it out. It won't be a problem, Gunnlaugur. OK?'

He nodded.

'How are you doing?' she asked, trying to inject a note of concern into her voice. She had to keep him sweet. She tried not to look at him as she sat beside him in the gloom. Ármann was bending over the man in the corner, apparently speaking to him.

'Just tired,' Gunnlaugur said after a pause. 'Terribly tired.'

She saw that he was still cradling his father's gun.

'Why don't you stand up? Try stretching a bit. That should wake you up.'

'Yes, maybe.'

He eased himself slowly to his feet, joints cracking, never letting go of his weapon.

Then he said indistinctly: 'Ármann . . . Why's he so close to the man? He's taking a huge risk. Helena, did you hear what I said? Can't you see?'

'He's only trying to talk to him. Relax.'

Ármann

He went back over to Gunnlaugur and Helena. He had switched on his torch again, placing it on the floor to shed a little light in the room while they were waiting for the late winter dawn.

He sensed that everything was returning to normal, the new day bringing new hope, as so often before.

Ármann couldn't wait to get back to town. The weekend had been well organized and one could safely say he had been looking forward to it, from that perspective. Of course, the weather had put a spanner in the works, but the end was in sight. Now they could go home. One thing was certain: he wouldn't miss Gunnlaugur. He'd be happy if he never saw his face again.

'Ármann.' Gunnlaugur broke in on his thoughts. 'Shouldn't we ... Shouldn't we go out and look for Daníel?' He sounded weary as he said it.

Ármann became acutely aware of his own tiredness at the thought of having to put up with Gunnlaugur questioning all his decisions. He hadn't had much time for the

RAGNAR JÓNASSON

guy before this trip but Gunnlaugur was the type whose worst qualities were exacerbated by travelling and being cooped up in enclosed spaces. A whole weekend with him had been far worse than Ármann would ever have imagined possible.

'There's no point, mate,' he said, striving for patience. 'You must understand that, surely?' He couldn't keep the edge out of his voice as he continued: 'You want to go out there? In these conditions? To look where, exactly? Do you want to die of exposure too?'

'He . . . You think he . . . ?'

'Sorry, no, of course I don't know that. I'm sure he'll make it. I didn't mean it like that. We just need to get back down to where there's a phone signal so we can ring for help. We're not members of a mountain-rescue team. At least, Helena and I aren't, but maybe you have some hidden talents that you haven't told us about?'

'What, me, no . . . He must have made it to the other hut.'

'Of course he must,' Ármann replied soothingly, though he didn't believe it. It was perfectly clear to him that no one could have survived the night out there.

Gunnlaugur sighed and lowered his head, as though he was becoming reconciled to the idea that there was nothing they could do. But then Ármann saw him start, his eyes widening in alarm.

'Ármann!' Gunnlaugur shouted, all the uncertainty vanishing from his voice, to be replaced by pure terror.

'What the hell . . . ?'

'Ármann, he's standing up!' Gunnlaugur said urgently and raised his gun. 'He's coming over, he's . . .'

Ármann froze for a split second, then realized that he needed to act fast. He was about to launch himself at Gunnlaugur but checked the impulse at the last minute, unwilling to put himself in the line of fire when he couldn't be sure that Gunnlaugur had sobered up yet. Instead, he sidestepped quickly, twisting as he did so to look over his shoulder at the man in the corner.

And then he heard a crack, the noise unbearably loud in that small space, as shattering and deafening as a yell from another world.

To his disbelief, Ármann saw that the shot had found its mark, and in that moment it felt as if the world had been smashed into a thousand pieces.

Gunnlaugur

The noise was so unreal that it took Gunnlaugur several seconds to comprehend what had happened; that he had actually fired his gun in the little hut.

The world went black in front of his eyes and at first he refused to believe the evidence of his own ears. What the hell had happened?

He closed his eyes in denial, refusing to deal with the consequences.

His reaction had been involuntary. He had aimed the gun the instant he saw that the man was on his feet and after that time had seemed to stand still. He had shouted at Ármann, seen the man start moving towards them in the half-light, hadn't even had time to ascertain whether his manner was threatening or if he was armed. He had simply panicked. Gunnlaugur had never before experienced such pure, unadulterated fear. But now that the shot had been fired, he was paralysed with horror. He didn't know yet if he had hit the man but even so it was too much for him. He couldn't believe he had actually pulled the trigger.

The shot must have gone astray; the alternative was unthinkable.

Gunnlaugur wasn't a hunter by nature and, despite his father's teaching, he barely knew how to handle a weapon. But somehow his instincts had taken charge and he had been quicker than ever before at aiming and firing.

He could still barely hear a thing, the echo of the bang drowning out every other sound, but then – suddenly – he thought he could hear screaming: a scream of terror contending with the ringing in his ears. His eyes were still tightly closed and he couldn't make out the words, just a confused babble of voices.

'Gunnlaugur!'

Was someone shouting his name?

'Gunnlaugur!'

Perhaps Ármann and Helena were both shouting at him. Were they warning him of imminent danger? Or were they reacting with horror to the fact that he'd . . .

That he'd . . .

He couldn't even form the words in his own mind. His brain refused to take in the enormity of what he'd done.

He thought his head was going to burst, the clamour echoing louder and louder until he couldn't bear it. No doubt only a few seconds had passed but he just couldn't take it any more.

He opened his eyes.

Helena

She watched the man clutching at his neck in the wake of the deafening explosion that had reverberated around the room as if a bomb had gone off. She had been uncomfortably close to Gunnlaugur when he fired, the gun almost by her ear, and for a moment she could hear nothing but a loud ringing.

Helena looked up, trying to make out the man's eyes in the dim light. His face wore an expression of utter astonishment.

Automatically, she moved towards Ármann and put her arms around him. He reached back a steadying arm to hold her close, and she watched the tragedy unfold from the safety of his embrace. Gunnlaugur was standing there rooted to the spot, his eyes screwed shut.

Then he flicked them open, dropping the gun on the floor as he did so. Helena braced herself for the impact to trigger another shot, but obviously it hadn't or she would have heard the bang. Her gaze returned automatically to the stranger. There was no question that he had been hit.

He staggered but it didn't even cross her mind to go over to him. Gunnlaugur didn't move either, just stood there gaping as if he had seen a ghost, unable to believe his own eyes. Ármann, meanwhile, maintained his habitual rock-like composure. He didn't make a move towards the injured man either but she got the feeling that his stillness was the result of a deliberate decision. With no one to help him, the man swayed a moment longer, then collapsed onto the floor, and now she could see the blood, dark red in the gloom.

The whole thing was so nightmarish that Helena allowed herself to hope that it really was a bad dream from which she would shortly wake up. She didn't say a word, but Ármann had yelled ineffectually at Gunnlaugur several times after he fired before lapsing into silence as well.

Shit, what the hell were they going to do?

Ármann

There was no point shouting.

Nothing was getting through.

Gunnlaugur stood there empty-handed, the gun on the floor, looking as if he had absented himself from the situation by escaping into some far corner of his mind.

The problem was that escape wasn't bloody possible.

Ármann tried to control his breathing. Now more than ever he needed to keep a cool head.

Helena was standing behind him, clinging to him, as if hiding.

Gunnlaugur had fatally injured the man; from the amount of blood there was no shadow of doubt about that. He'd succeeded in getting them all into a total fucking mess.

Ármann couldn't think more than a few seconds ahead; everything was a blur, the future didn't exist, although he tried his damnedest not to lose his concentration.

He knew he had to save what could be salvaged. After all, he had hit rock bottom once before and managed to emerge in one piece. This time it was Gunnlaugur's fault, but regardless of who was to blame, it would be Ármann's job to clean up after him.

He would have to save Gunnlaugur's skin in order to get himself and Helena out of trouble.

Thank God Daníel was out of the picture. That made things a little more straightforward.

Ármann would happily have thrown Gunnlaugur to the wolves but, sadly, in this case it wouldn't solve the problem.

There, on that winter morning, in a godforsaken hut in the highlands, a man was bleeding to death in front of their eyes. As Ármann was pretty sure he was beyond their aid, he reckoned it was safer to keep their distance. He needed time to think.

There weren't many options. Any minute now they were going to find themselves with a dead body on their hands.

He wondered if it had come home to Gunnlaugur yet that he had killed a man.

Gunnlaugur

The gun was lying on the floor and so was the man.

He might still be showing signs of life but Gunnlaugur couldn't move. He just stood there, rigid, watching, as if the situation had nothing to do with him, though of course he knew better. He had never been brave and nothing had changed there. Yet in spite of that he had found the courage – or recklessness – to fire.

Had the man really been a threat to him?

Or had Gunnlaugur momentarily lost his grip, with devastating consequences?

What would happen now? What would happen if the man didn't make it?

Although the stranger had stopped moving, Gunnlaugur let himself hope that things weren't quite as bad as they appeared; that the wound wasn't fatal and the stranger would survive . . .

There was nothing he could do now but hope.

Helena

'What are we going to do?'

Helena murmured her question to Ármann, pressed close to his side, so Gunnlaugur wouldn't hear. She could hardly even hear herself, the aftershock of the shot was so great.

Ármann turned his head. 'We wait. I need to think.'

She got a glimpse of his face for the first time since Gunnlaugur had fired.

Ármann's solid bulk had felt rock-like but the expression in his eyes told a different story. He was scared. She knew that look too well: he was terrified.

She consoled herself with the thought that Ármann really came into his own under pressure, though that might not be enough this time.

What disturbed her more was that it wasn't only fear she had read in his eyes. She knew him too well. There was no mistaking the fact that he was furiously, frighteningly, angry. And that's when he was liable to make his worst mistakes.

Ármann

'It'll be all right,' he told Helena, trying to steady the tremor in his voice. 'OK? It'll be all right.'

He turned his attention back to Gunnlaugur.

'Gunnlaugur,' he said again, raising his voice. There was no reaction. But he couldn't stop himself; he needed to vent his rage: 'What the fuck have you done? Listen to me! You've killed him.'

Ármann lowered his eyes again to the victim. There was no doubt he'd been mortally wounded. That stupid bastard Gunnlaugur's aim had been better than Ármann would ever have dreamed. And now the useless piece of shit was standing there saying nothing, doing nothing, with no answers.

Ármann went on furiously: 'What are you going to do now, eh? What are you going to do? What were you thinking of? For fuck's sake! He was completely harmless . . .'

It was futile.

Gunnlaugur was somewhere beyond his reach, but, on second thoughts, perhaps that wasn't such a bad

thing. He wouldn't be any use to them; quite the opposite, in fact. At least if he was out of it, he wouldn't get in
their way.

When Ármann turned his attention back to Helena, he
saw how distressed she was. Of course, that was to be
expected. She didn't say a word but he knew exactly what
she was thinking.

It would be up to *them* to clean up his mess and sort
this out.

They had two alternatives, but it was pretty obvious
which they would choose. Either notify the police the
moment they got down from the highlands, or help
Gunnlaugur hide his tracks.

Ármann wasn't sure which course Gunnlaugur would
choose for himself, if he had any say.

He was a lawyer, after all, and no doubt his record had
been pretty unblemished up to now. His first reaction, once
he'd got his bearings, would presumably be to hand himself
in and confess to everything. Plead self-defence, perhaps.
Of course Ármann and Helena could support that version
of events, even if it was untrue. Gunnlaugur hadn't been
in any danger; nothing could justify what he had done. Alter-
natively, Ármann and Helena could tell the simple truth, that
Gunnlaugur had panicked and murdered a man and that
there were no extenuating circumstances. Ármann toyed
for a moment with the idea of sacrificing Gunnlaugur and
watching him suffer. But regrettably it wasn't a viable option.

They would have to lie – or omit to tell the truth, at
least – and help Gunnlaugur avoid a prison sentence.

And yes, sure, although Gunnlaugur was a lawyer with

an 'unblemished record' in one sense, Ármann knew that wasn't the whole story. He knew about the rape, about when Gunnlaugur – drunk, of course – had forced himself on a girl at a party. Ármann had never discussed this with Gunnlaugur but he was aware of it, as most of their group of friends were, because Gunnlaugur had let it slip himself once when his drinking was out of control. For some reason the girl had never pressed charges. It was possible Gunnlaugur had bought her silence . . . at least, it was clear that in his case outward appearances were deceptive; he had a dark side that he did his best to keep under wraps. It was this that convinced Ármann it might just be possible to persuade him that the only reasonable course of action now was to behave as if nothing had happened. He mustn't give in to his conscience. The deed was done; the man was lying unconscious on the floor, perhaps he had already crossed to the other side. What mattered now was to save what could be salvaged from the situation.

'Gunnlaugur, can you hear me?'

Again, he might have been talking to a brick wall.

'Gunnlaugur, he's dead, you can see that. We've got to do something.' Ármann went over and stood face to face with Gunnlaugur, putting his hands warily on his shoulders. Locking eyes with him, he asked again: 'Can you hear me?'

Finally, Gunnlaugur responded. He blinked, then squinted around him, as if dazed.

'I just don't know . . . don't know what happened . . .' he said, his voice catching on a sob. That's all they needed,

Ármann thought sourly, for the useless prick to start bawling his eyes out.

He tightened his grip on the other man's shoulders. 'Gunnlaugur, we'll sort it out, OK?'

Finally, Gunnlaugur gathered his wits sufficiently to react. 'You what? What did you say?'

Ármann raised his voice. No doubt the retort of the gun was still ringing in Gunnlaugur's ears. 'We'll sort it out.'

'Sort it out? What are you talking about?' Gunnlaugur exclaimed with a rush of anger. 'Can't you see him lying there? How are we supposed to sort that out?'

Ármann lowered his arms and took a couple of steps backwards, all the while careful to keep well away from the still figure on the floor.

'I've got some suggestions,' Ármann said in a clear, level voice. He shot a glance at Helena, who gave a curt nod, obviously unwilling to take part in the conversation.

'Suggestions?' Gunnlaugur asked, sounding both angry and bewildered.

'Yes, firstly, we could . . .'

'*Suggestions?*' Gunnlaugur said again, outraged. 'There's nothing we can do. We'll just have to get out of here and ring the police.'

'Are you absolutely sure about that?'

'Sure? Of course I'm sure! What are you planning to do, just leave the man lying there? And what am I supposed to do? Flee the country? I . . . I have to take the consequences, you know; stand trial for what I've done.'

'None of that legal bullshit now, Gunnlaugur. This is

neither the time nor place. Stand trial? You've got your friends here to back you up, OK?'

Gunnlaugur nodded. 'Yes,' he said doubtfully.

It occurred to Ármann that the choice of words had been unfortunate, that 'friends' had rung a little false. It couldn't be helped. Right now they all needed to be on the same team, to act as friends. Afterwards, he was confident that Gunnlaugur would vanish from their lives for good.

But Gunnlaugur hadn't finished: 'All the same, you know, we can't . . . We . . .'

'What can't we do, eh? Can we let you go to prison? Is that what you want? Frankly, mate, I couldn't care less, so if that's what you want, we can make the decision here and now. Obviously there's nothing we can do for the poor sod, so we'll just hang on a bit longer. The weather's improving. It'll be daylight soon. I trust myself to find my way back to the lodge then. We should be able to let the police know quite quickly, as soon as we get a phone signal. OK?' He glared at Gunnlaugur, his gaze locked with his. 'We'll look after you until the police can come and take you into custody. Or do you lawyers merit some kind of special treatment?'

All the remaining colour seemed to drain from Gunnlaugur's face, as if only now was he taking in the full gravity of what he'd done.

Gunnlaugur

He had never felt like this before. It was like being somewhere in the grey area between sleep and waking, although he was in fact wide awake; caught between imagination and reality, perhaps because he knew somewhere in the back of his mind that the reality was more terrible than anything his imagination could conjure up. He couldn't face what he had done; all he wanted was to disappear, even if only to fall asleep for a little while and allow himself a brief respite.

But when he closed his eyes the body appeared before his mind's eye and he couldn't think about anything but the man he had murdered.

Murdered.

The word echoed in his head, as if he were hearing it for the first time. He had taken a human life and nothing would ever be the same again. Inadvertently, his thoughts had already turned to his future. There would never be room for anything else in his mind. This deed would be the beginning and end of everything. Could he ever go back to work, just turn up on Monday morning, bold as brass, as if nothing had happened? Perhaps he would have to go into the office, try to tough it out, go on with his life, but he knew that every minute, every second, would be an ordeal. For an instant he pictured his desk with its mundane stacks of files that had seemed to suck all the colour out of existence. Yesterday he had been dreading having to go back to work because he was so bored, so stuck in a rut, but now he would have given anything – in fact everything – for a chance to rewind, to be the same old Gunnlaugur, experience the same old tedium at the office; right now that would be his idea of bliss. He could see the beauty in the monotony and, above all, the beauty in his innocence.

He opened his eyes and took in his surroundings.

He was vaguely aware that the others were trying to talk to him but he was locked in the turmoil of his own thoughts.

He had been brought up to do the right thing, to obey his parents, to perform well, never to cause any ripples, and he had succeeded, almost too well. Sometimes he'd got the feeling he was missing out on life, that he had missed out on all the adventures of youth, but now he was becoming acquainted with extremes, with a terrible atrocity that had converted him in one fell swoop from a good person into a bad one.

His head felt as if it were bursting, he could still hear the shot echoing in the distance, again and again, his ears were buzzing, and perhaps it was this that intensified the sensation of being trapped in a kind of hell from which there was no return.

He couldn't stop his thoughts from straying to how other people would see him from now on. He would be denounced as a murderer. Everything positive he had achieved in his life would be blotted out, as if with the single stroke of a pen. A single horrific crime. Would he ever be able to look his friends and colleagues in the eye again? He would be condemned to be alone for ever, and . . .

And, yes, there was the prospect of prison. For some reason that hadn't even occurred to him at first. He felt the sweat breaking out all over his body and his heart pounding. Prison. Obviously that was where he was headed. He couldn't even bear to think about being locked up.

But there was a sense in which he was innocent, even in the eyes of the law. His action had been involuntary, partly in self-defence. Honestly. All right, not directly; not quite directly, but almost. He had been afraid for his life and spontaneously reacted in this terrible way.

Trying to shut out the noise his friends were making, he drew a deep breath, then took a step forward, but it felt as if the floor of the hut was sloping down and he was falling. He was hit by a wave of vertigo. His sense of balance had deserted him, his mind was racing: the dead man, the noise of the shot, his future . . .

The feeling of chaos intensified, his vertigo got the better of him and, admitting defeat, he sank to the floor.

'Gunnlaugur.' Ármann's voice broke through his churn-ing thoughts. 'Gunnlaugur, are you all right?'

He shook his head.

'It's over,' he quavered. 'It's all over.'

'Easy now.' The customary authoritative note was back in Ármann's voice. He was taking charge and this time Gunnlaugur would have to accept the fact.

'I . . .' He trailed off, unable to find the right words, incapable of finishing another sentence.

'It's a bloody mess,' Ármann said harshly. 'A bloody mess, but we'll find a way of dealing with it. Our first job is to get rid of the body.' He sighed.

When he tried to nod his agreement, Gunnlaugur dis-covered that the last of his strength had drained away. He just sat there on the floor, gazing helplessly up at his friend. And now he felt as if Ármann was the only one who could save him from sinking into the abyss.

Helena

Get rid of the body, Ármann had said.

The words sounded unreal, as if they had nothing to do with her.

Shivering with the cold though she was, in spite of her thick clothing, she felt an overwhelming compulsion to run out of the door into the icy morning.

She could feel her breath coming fast and shallow, her heart pounding in her chest with the stress.

She averted her eyes from the body on the floor as she mustn't let herself wonder who the man was and whether he had a family or if anyone would miss him. Yet she couldn't stop herself because it was clear that she was going to have to take part in covering up Gunnlaugur's crime and therefore share the responsibility for preventing the poor man's family from ever finding out what had happened to him.

'How?' she asked, without really meaning to. She just had to say something to dispel the unbearable thoughts, if only for a moment.

Ármann turned to her, looking puzzled. 'What?'

She hesitated, then said: 'How are you planning to get rid of the body?'

It was his turn to pause. Perhaps he hadn't fully thought it through. 'We . . .'

'No way! Absolutely no way!' Gunnlaugur cried, his voice shrill and trembling.

'Leave it to us,' Ármann snapped. He turned back to Helena: 'We could . . . we could carry it,' he suggested uncertainly. 'Find somewhere to dump it.'

'Like where?'

'A fissure or something. I can't immediately think of any in the area, but . . .'

An uncomfortable silence fell.

'We could burn down the hut,' Ármann said suddenly.

'Burn it down?' she exclaimed. 'Are you joking?'

It would never have occurred to her and she found the idea gruesome, to say the least. Not just to set the hut alight but to burn a body inside it . . . She would never have imagined herself being an accomplice to a crime like that and she wasn't even sure she was capable of it. Yet she would have to play along. They were in this together.

'Why the fuck did you have to do it, Gunnlaugur?' She rounded on him, fighting back the urge to launch herself at him. 'For Christ's sake, why? You've ruined everything!'

He stared at her like a chastened child. 'I . . . I . . .'

'We should never have brought you along.'

'Helena, this is pointless,' Ármann warned. 'You need to calm down.'

Gunnlaugur didn't speak.

'Never! We should never have brought you along,' she ranted on, unable to stop herself. 'I told you, Ármann – didn't I?'

Ármann nodded.

Helena continued: 'I told you we shouldn't bring a bloody rapist along!'

She saw Gunnlaugur flinch.

'I never meant to –' He broke off and Helena glared at him, waiting for him to finish. 'I had no intention of raping you. Really, I didn't, Helena. I was just drunk and behaving like an idiot.'

And you still are, she wanted to say.

'I wasn't talking about that,' she snapped.

She saw the way his expression changed from surprise to horror.

'I'm talking about the girl you raped years ago, at a party. Remember?'

She had never tackled him about it before and hadn't intended to mention it now. What's more, she was sure neither Ármann nor Daníel had ever raised the incident with him.

Gunnlaugur seemed to have been rendered speechless. Finally, after a long, awkward silence, he said in a choked voice: 'You can't bring that up now, OK? Not now, please, Helena, I . . . Can't you see what's just happened? I can't . . .'

She thought it over and took a deep breath. Of course, this was a totally inappropriate moment, but she felt compelled to get it off her chest. The incident wasn't any of her business, not directly, but she had heard the story, pretty much first hand. And it was plain from his expression that he couldn't deny the accusation.

'After this weekend I'm never speaking to you again, Gunnlaugur. It was a terrible mistake to invite you along, but – God knows why – Ármann wants to try and help you – to drag you out of the pit you've dug for yourself. But, just so you know – I'm not getting involved.'

'I . . .'

'Don't waste your breath denying it. We all know what happened. We all know what you're like.'

Gunnlaugur clasped his head in his hands. 'Daníel,' he muttered weakly. 'Why isn't Daníel here?'

'Why, do you think he would save your arse?' Ármann said coldly.

Helena still hadn't recovered her composure. Her heart was racing, her agitation rising. This is how she had felt when she heard about Víkingur. She supposed she had never got over the trauma. Perhaps that's why her anger was always so close to boiling over.

Unable to stop herself, she screamed at Gunnlaugur: 'Daníel's dead, can't you get that into your thick head? He must have died of exposure by now. We can't do anything for him – *you* can't do anything for him. Because you can be sure he's not going to rise from the dead, any more than the man lying on the floor. No one's going to save you. It would have been better if you'd died too!'

Ármann

'That's enough,' Ármann said. He had often seen Helena worked up, but rarely like this. 'We all need to get a grip. We need to think logically so we can figure out what to do.'

'Daníel would . . .' Gunnlaugur said, but the words petered out and it was impossible to guess what he had been intending to say.

'Of course, we hope he's all right,' Ármann said soothingly. 'Helena's being far too negative. We have to be positive.'

'Positive?' Helena cut in. 'There's a dead man lying on the floor in front of us, in case you hadn't noticed.'

'Helena . . .' Ármann snapped, something he rarely did with her.

He closed his eyes, breathing in the cold, dank air, tainted now with the iron smell of blood. Then he scanned the interior of the hut. In spite of the growing daylight outside, it was still dim in here, the snow on the windows trapping the twilight inside. Gunnlaugur had got to his feet and taken a step or two towards the door. As if, consciously or not, he wanted an easy escape route, although naturally the idea of escape was an illusion: the hut might as well have been a prison. Helena, meanwhile, was standing at Ármann's side, though not as close to him as before.

He frowned at her, fixing her eyes with his, wanting to convey, though not with words, how urgent it was for the two of them to stand united.

'Burn down . . . What you said before, about burning down the hut . . .' Gunnlaugur began.

'Yes?'

'What would that achieve?'

'How do you mean?'

'They'd still find the body, wouldn't they? Or at least the remains, or . . . ?'

Ármann smiled grimly. At last Gunnlaugur had begun to grasp the gravity of the situation and was showing signs of playing along. His question was a perfectly valid one.

'Probably. I simply don't know. I've never set fire to any bodies before. Have you got a better suggestion?'

'Er, no . . . I don't know what –' Gunnlaugur broke off, then went on: 'I was just thinking, if they find the remains, even if no one can tell who it was, they'll start searching . . .' He didn't finish.

'Searching for the murderer, you mean?'

Gunnlaugur nodded.

'Right. But there's nothing we can do about that. You'll just have to live with it, Gunnlaugur. You know that, don't you? We're going to help you – or at least *try* to help you – hold on to your freedom, but your conscience is your problem, mate. You'll have to learn to live with the fact you're a murderer.'

'And a fucking rapist,' Helena said in a low voice.

Gunnlaugur

No one had ever called him that before, not aloud.

Of course, he had suspected there were rumours about what he had done, although he'd hoped there weren't, and that the anonymous letters, bad as they were, had been sent to him and him alone.

It was all too much: the knowledge that *other people knew*, on top of the terrible mess he had just got himself into.

Perhaps none of it mattered any more. Perhaps, without realizing it, he had already been a social outcast and the murder wouldn't make much difference.

Maybe he should just hand himself in and relieve Ármann and Helena of their dilemma.

But then he thought about the consequences, the difference between these two crimes.

The rape was one person's word against another's, and he had absolutely no intention of confessing to it, however guilty he knew himself to be. They would never be able to prove anything against him.

But if he admitted to manslaughter, there was every chance that he would end up in prison.

And he'd never be able to bear that.

What Ármann had said was right: *Gunnlaugur would have to face up to the fact that he now had murder on his conscience too.*

At the same time it hit him that any idea of being saved by Daníel was an illusion. He felt in his bones that his friend was dead – Daníel, his oldest friend, who had always looked out for him.

He felt a lump forming in his throat but there was no time for that now. He had to focus. He would mourn him later. Instead, he coughed and asked: 'How are you planning to set fire to it?'

Ármann was brought up short. It seemed he hadn't considered the practicalities. 'This is nothing but a primitive shelter,' he admitted after a pause. 'With no means of heating. No gas or fuel of any kind . . .'

'Have you got matches or a lighter or . . . ?' As Gunnlaugur asked this, it felt as if someone else was saying the words. He couldn't believe he was actually plotting to commit arson, but it was almost as if one crime excused the other. He had killed a man and so it wouldn't make much difference if he added arson – as long as he wasn't found out. He would have to deal with his conscience later.

Ármann nodded. 'Yes, I always carry matches in my backpack, that's not the problem. But we must be able to find . . .'

'There's a bottle of barbecue lighter fluid in the corner, I noticed it yesterday,' Helena said doubtfully, as if she was reluctant to help but had decided to in spite of herself.

'Yes, right, that could work, I suppose.' Then Ármann burst out, after a short silence: 'Fucking, fucking hell. Why did you have to go and shoot him, Gunnlaugur?'

Helena

She had such a vivid memory of the first time she met Víkingur.

She had been freezing cold, like now. Yet the memory itself was warm. She always felt better when she thought back to that Monday in front of the university building. A typical, miserable autumn Monday, one of those piercingly cold September days that was more reminiscent of the winter to come than the newly departed summer. She had been distracted, still unfamiliar with the campus, searching for a different building from the one where she had most of her lectures. And he had come over to talk to her, apparently sensing that she needed help, and before she knew it he had invited her to go for a coffee. 'There's no point standing out here, let's get into the warm.' She didn't remember his exact words but he'd said something along those lines, and she had known immediately that the conversation marked the beginning of something important.

Every aspect of that Monday was enveloped in a glow,

even the dreary September chill, the crushing heaviness of autumn. No doubt the leaves covering the ground had been soggy and tattered, but in her memory they had carpeted the pavement like props on a stage, for a play in which the two of them – Helena and Víkingur – were the protagonists.

It was comforting to lose oneself in the memory of that day, blocking out the noise of Ármann and Gunnlaugur's voices, the horror and shadows in the hut that they were now planning to burn to the ground. The whole thing felt surreal.

But it all came back to Víkingur.

It had always been about him, all along.

Ármann

'OK, let's try it,' he said, trying to sound firm.

'What, right now?' Gunnlaugur asked.

Ármann hesitated, then said: 'Yes, I reckon. Now.' He glanced at the window. As far as he could tell, the weather had improved, though it was still snowing. Nevertheless, he was confident he could find his way back.

He was less confident about their plan, though. On reflection, it was almost certainly a terrible mistake . . .

Would a half-empty bottle of lighter fluid really be enough to send the whole hut up in flames? And surely it would be possible to identify the body even after it had been burnt? By the dental records, for example? Perhaps they should try something different. He drew a deep breath.

'What about him – the man?' Gunnlaugur asked, lowering his gaze to the still figure on the floor.

'How do you mean?'

'If we set fire to the hut, we'll never find out who he was. Won't we need to know, so we're prepared? I mean, people will be looking for him. I just . . .'

'Are you completely out of your mind, Gunnlaugur? What are you planning to do? Take a photo with your phone to appease your conscience or something?'

'No, I didn't mean that, I'm just worried . . .'

'Worry about yourself instead. You killed the man. It wasn't us. Do what you like, OK? I've had enough. Helena and I are going.'

Ármann met Helena's eye and she nodded.

'We'll find our way back,' she said. 'No worries.'

Ármann saw the fear taking hold of Gunnlaugur.

'No, I can't do this alone!' he cried. 'You've got to help me!'

Ármann had never heard Gunnlaugur sound so desperate before. In different circumstances he might have experienced a sense of schadenfreude but now he found it deeply uncomfortable.

'For fuck's sake, man, we're trying to help you. Just stop your whining.'

'All right.' Gunnlaugur sniffed.

'To tell the truth, I haven't a clue how we're supposed to sort this out. Maybe the only way is to dispose of the body. It's just a question of how . . . We can probably lift him between us, you and me.' Ármann gave Gunnlaugur an appraising glance. 'We're unlikely to run into anyone out here, but . . .'

'Hang on, what about the blood on the floor? Won't we *have* to set fire to the hut?'

There was a new, unsettling note in Gunnlaugur's voice. He seemed to be veering between a pathetic state of indecision and a sudden cold ruthlessness. Ármann got

the impression that Gunnlaugur could actually be dangerous in the right – or wrong – circumstances. After all, he
had shot a man at close range – perhaps deliberately.

'It wouldn't be a good idea if it went wrong, you know,'
Ármann reasoned. 'Then we'd be in a mess. It might be
more sensible to try to get rid of all the evidence here
first, then to dispose of the body. Nobody knows he was
here, so there's not much risk of anyone putting two and
two together.'

Gunnlaugur nodded.

'OK, er, you're in charge, Ármann. I've never been
involved in anything like this before.'

Ármann almost lost it then. It seemed he would never
be free of his past. No doubt Gunnlaugur was referring,
directly or indirectly, to his former life in Copenhagen.
Whenever Ármann was with his old friends and acquaintances, he was aware of its shadow hanging over him. But
the truth was that he had never before been involved in
having to decide whether it was a good idea to burn a
building to the ground.

Still, the situation called for a cool head, so he mustn't
let himself be riled by Gunnlaugur's comment.

'We'll take the body outside, then do our best to clean
up after Gunnlaugur,' Ármann said with sudden decision,
aware that time was working against them.

Gunnlaugur

He would have to trust them. What choice did he have? But he found himself wondering what he really knew about Ármann or Helena, about how their minds worked. The connection had always been through Daníel, and deep down Gunnlaugur didn't trust them.

Sure, he'd always had a thing for Helena, but he'd never been able to work her out. Anyway, she could be depended on to take Ármann's side in everything, and there was no telling what Ármann might be capable of.

Ordinarily, Gunnlaugur would never have associated with a man like him as they were such different types. For all his cheeriness and outgoing nature, Ármann could be a bit of a lout at times – borderline dangerous, in fact. It seemed the only person he really respected was Helena. She could control – even dominate – him.

Yet here they were, with the roles completely reversed, with Ármann innocent and Gunnlaugur mired in guilt. He had killed a man. The whole thing was so topsy-turvy that it was absurd. It should have been Ármann standing

over a bloody corpse with a gun in his hands and Gunnlaugur defending him in court – though in truth he
doubted his colleagues would have entrusted him with
such a major case.

He was gripped by the vague, unsettling notion that he
was being led into a trap, but he couldn't work out why.
He had no reason for this totally unfounded suspicion.
They weren't playing with him; on the contrary, they were
helping him. If they did nothing, he would be in an even
worse mess; he might even have to stand trial. That would
be the end of his life as he knew it.

Yet he couldn't quite rid himself of his disquiet, of the
suspicion that they were hiding something from him,
ludicrous though the idea was. He was the one who had
pulled the trigger. That wasn't in doubt. And the man was
definitely dead, wasn't he?

'Are you quite sure he's . . . ?'

Ármann finished the question for him: 'Dead? What
the hell do you think? You shot him in the throat at point-
blank range.'

Gunnlaugur made a choked noise.

'He's not moving,' Ármann went on. 'There's blood
everywhere. Why don't you check his pulse? Because I'm
not doing it for you.'

'What? No, no, it . . .'

'Well, *you* shot him.'

Gunnlaugur took a step backwards, unable to face
going anywhere near the body, though he knew that he
and Ármann would have to touch it if they were to carry
it out of the hut together.

'Going somewhere, Gunnlaugur?'

This time it was Helena who asked, and there was an odd look on her face, almost as if she was pleased with the way things were developing. But that was impossible. Gunnlaugur knew he must be careful not to let his imagination run away with him. He had to stay calm; he couldn't afford to lose his grip like this.

As it was, he would face a prison sentence and his reputation would be in tatters. He would be barred from practising as a lawyer after being found guilty of a crime of this magnitude. Not that it would make much difference, as no one in their right mind would employ him ever again.

He must push away these paranoid imaginings and confront the facts.

He had committed a terrible crime.

And at this moment Helena and Ármann were his best – his only – friends.

Helena

For her own part, she hardly cared how things turned out, but she would have to support Ármann as well as she could and, sadly, that would mean supporting Gunnlaugur too.

The truth was that if everything turned out badly, she herself would probably get off scot-free, as Ármann could be relied on to protect her.

All she had to do was keep her head and get through this as best she could. To distract herself, she thought about the flat she had just bought in the city centre. Although she hadn't settled in properly yet, she could hardly wait to be snuggled up in her bed there. The next step was to buy a sofa and some furniture for the kitchen. That was her plan for this week.

Everything had been going so well until Gunnlaugur went and killed that man.

What hurt most bitterly was the thought that he would walk free. It occurred to her that if she wanted to see justice done, one option would be to get in touch with the girl he had raped and encourage her to press charges by offering to help her. It was evident what sort of person Gunnlaugur was underneath and even though the incident in question had nothing to do with Helena, the fact was that shits like him deserved to get their comeuppance, in one way or another.

Ármann

Glancing at the window again, Ármann saw the morning light filtering more strongly now through the snow on the glass.

Instinct told him they would have to work fast. He wasn't sure how it would all pan out in the end. At this moment he was being driven entirely by the urge for self-preservation. That and the need to protect Helena, as always.

He thought about Daníel, lost out there on the moors, surely gone to meet his ancestors by now. Yet Ármann was aware that it could take time for someone to die of exposure, longer than many people would have believed possible, as the human body was incredibly tough when put to the test. At least there was no chance of their stumbling across him. God alone knew where his body was now, lying among the drifts, in the place where he must have looked on the darkness for the last time, unable to believe that no one was coming to rescue him.

That was the worst part, Ármann thought, his mind

flying back over the years: lying there, alone and abandoned, feeling your hope fading.

Ármann himself had resolved long ago to take his fate into his own hands, to be an agent, not a victim, and even though he hadn't always managed to stick to it, this principle had generally served him well. Helena was like him in that respect.

'Right, shall we get cracking then?' he said to Gunnlaugur.

Gunnlaugur had backed towards the door, as if to put as much distance as possible between himself and them, between himself and the dead body. If Ármann hadn't known better – hadn't known that Gunnlaugur was a terrible coward and had no idea where they were – he might have wondered if Gunnlaugur was positioning himself in order to make a run for it. But no one except Helena would have a hope in hell of getting back to the lodge from here without Ármann to guide them.

Gunnlaugur

The thought of helping Ármann carry the body out of the hut to dispose of it somewhere made Gunnlaugur sick to the stomach.

'Hey, did you hear me?' Ármann asked sharply. But it was as if Gunnlaugur couldn't process the words, as if his body was refusing to listen.

'Yes, I'm coming,' he said at last, without meaning it, standing rooted to the spot for a moment, before shrinking even further back to press himself against the closed door. He stared wildly at Ármann and Helena in turn, convinced that they were moving towards him, that the walls were closing in on him. He had to get outside, to catch his breath, to fill his lungs with oxygen and break free somehow from this hideous nightmare.

'Gunnlaugur! Gunnlaugur!'

He wasn't even sure which of them was calling; perhaps both at once.

Perhaps no one.

'Gunnlaugur!'

Then the little hut seemed to shake; this miserable, freezing hovel that had provided the frame for an unspeakable crime, its thin walls the backdrop, the wailing wind the orchestra, and the director lurking somewhere unseen in the shadows.

It was a disorientating sensation. Was it his imagination, this shaking, or could they be experiencing an earthquake on top of everything else?

Again, he felt a violent tremor running through the hut. This definitely wasn't his imagination.

He tried to gather his wits and focus on what was happening.

Helena

'There's ... there's someone knocking on the door,' Helena said breathlessly, turning to Ármann for confirmation. She was uncertain, her ears still ringing, the tension so tightly wound in the hut that she could well have misheard.

Ármann nodded, and for the first time she saw alarm in his eyes. *He* wasn't supposed to be frightened.

'I think so . . .'

'Gunnlaugur! Move! There's someone outside,' she said, raising her voice.

Belatedly, Gunnlaugur seemed to register what was happening, though surely he couldn't have failed to hear the noise and feel the jarring impact of the blows, with his back pressed to the door like that?

Yet he didn't budge.

'Move!' Helena repeated, though it was the last thing she wanted.

A sort of menacing equilibrium had been achieved between the three of them, driven by hate, anger, fear and self-preservation. Now she was afraid that this precarious balance would be destroyed. If her suspicion proved correct, she couldn't even begin to imagine how it would all end.

Then, as if he had been given a violent shove, Gunnlaugur lurched forwards and almost fell as the door opened inwards behind him.

Helena turned her head away.

She didn't want to know the truth. Not yet.

Daniel

The door wouldn't budge. With the last reserves of his strength, he managed to shove it open an inch or two, but there seemed to be some solid weight blocking it from the other side.

Were they trying to stop him getting in? After the thoughts that had been raging through his head all night, it wouldn't surprise him . . . He had been trying to piece it all together as he battled the snow, trying to work out what was really going on.

Perhaps the suspicion had always been there underneath, in his subconscious; he just hadn't confronted it.

It seemed impossible that he had found his way back here alive. His fingers were numb; the cold and the fear had almost killed him. After leaving Helena it had only been a matter of minutes before he felt himself becoming increasingly disorientated by the swirling flakes, unable to work out if he was walking in a straight line, probably going in circles. The terrain had offered no clues; any potential landmarks were blurred by the drifts.

Salvation was just an illusion, and the never-ending fields of snow felt like a final resting place, and perhaps that was the way things were supposed to end for him ... Phantom huts kept looming out of the blizzard.

He could feel the cold creeping into his very core.

At some point he had fallen and lain there, ready to succumb to exhaustion. It was easier to give up.

Then he had started walking, almost crawling to begin with, letting instinct guide the way. There was no chance of working out the direction, no hope of finding out where he was. The doubt had been growing in his mind that the other hut even existed. Why had he agreed to go out into the snow? It was almost as if Helena and Ármann hadn't really given him any choice. Why had they wanted to send him out into the storm?

As he floundered on, sinking with every step into the soft, fresh drifts, praying that he was retracing his steps, he kept hoping he would stumble across Helena, so she wouldn't be left behind, injured and helpless. Every now and then he had shouted out her name, but the storm seemed to snatch the sound away and however hard he strained his ears he couldn't hear a reply. In the end he'd had no thoughts left but the need to stay alive. The extraordinary part was how stubborn the will to live turned out to be when put to the ultimate test. Daníel had been astonished by his own determination. He had come close to collapsing with exhaustion, but by some miracle – and pure luck – he had found his way back.

He had found a small stream, hoping it was the one he had seen before, and then he had noticed that the weather was clearing a little; although the wind was still gusting, the snow had stopped coming down so thickly. His optimism had grown still further with the first grey rim of dawn in the eastern sky. And then he had seen it: the square shape of a hut on the horizon, dwarfed by the distance.

Now that safety lay within his grasp, he couldn't believe that he couldn't get in. Frantically, he flung his entire weight at the door and it opened inwards with such suddenness that he almost fell into the hut.

He scraped the snow from his face and eyelashes with his frozen hands. He was standing behind a figure he realized was Gunnlaugur but he couldn't see clearly into the dimly lit room beyond. He threw his arms around his friend, having never felt so happy to see him or indeed any other human being in his life. All his suspicions melted away before the overwhelming realization that he was safe, among friends. The snow was stopping and soon he would be back in civilization, at his parents' house in Reykjavík, and hopefully, as soon as possible after that, in London again, with his girlfriend.

Then, his elation draining away, he remembered Helena.

Of course, they wouldn't be able to go home until they had searched for her in the vain hope that it wasn't too late to save her.

Ármann

In his initial shock, when he heard the hammering on the
door and realized that someone was standing outside, of
course his first thought should have been Daníel.

But Ármann had been utterly convinced that Daníel
had lost his life in the storm. It was impossible to believe
for one minute that a wimp like him could have survived
in such extreme conditions.

Yet this was the reality Ármann was now forced to
confront.

There he stood, that poor excuse for an actor, that
poor excuse for a human being, showing far more signs
of life than the man on the floor, that was certain.

Daníel stood behind Gunnlaugur for a moment,
hugging him, then seemed to be trying to push him
out of the way so he could get properly inside, into
shelter.

The icy wind came gusting through the open door.
Ármann shivered, but the problems facing him now were
far more serious than a cold draught. It had been bad

enough trying to cope with Gunnlaugur and the body on the floor, but now he had Daníel to contend with too. And he was bound to present the biggest problem, for a variety of reasons.

'Daníel,' he said quietly, but the word seemed to echo around the hut, as if dropped into a moment of absolute silence.

Gunnlaugur finally stepped aside, and Daníel gasped. 'I . . . I thought I wasn't going to make it, I . . . Helena, we've got to . . .'

The words died on his lips. He was staring, blankly, at Helena.

Ármann, glancing sideways, saw that she didn't even flinch, just returned his stare.

A long, fraught silence followed, which Ármann was reluctant to break. He was racking his brains about how to solve the riddle that had just presented itself and work out a way of dispelling the tension that now filled the hut.

'I thought you were injured,' Daníel said, after a stunned pause. 'I thought you were lying out there in the snow. Alone.'

Ármann could hear how heavily Daníel was breathing, see his expression gradually changing as his eyes narrowed with suspicion. The door was still open, snowflakes whirling inside.

Ármann looked at Helena again. She was just standing there, not saying a word.

'I thought you were injured?' Daníel repeated. 'I've

been desperately worried about you. I thought you'd die of exposure out there . . .'

And now, finally, Helena spoke.

'Like Víkingur, you mean?'

Helena

She hadn't meant to say it, but she hadn't been able to stop herself. The words had come of their own accord when she met Daníel's gaze. *Like Víkingur, you mean?*

How the hell had he managed to survive the storm?

She had underestimated him. She would never have believed he had the physical or mental strength to survive out there.

And now she had gone and dragged Víkingur's name into it, the name that had been hovering unspoken behind all their talk this weekend.

Daníel didn't immediately respond.

But she could see his shock, see his brain working. In spite of his ordeal, he was beginning to piece it together. A succession of emotions crossed his face, first amazement, then – yes – fear, and finally fury. But perhaps she was reading too much into his expressions and seeing only what she wanted to see, as it was hard to work out where imagination ended and reality began. She was miserably cold and exhausted. All she wanted now was to get out of here. Her plans had gone awry, but it couldn't be helped. Everything had its time.

Amazement, fear and fury.

Yes.

She derived some small consolation from watching it dawn on Daníel. His eyes were fixed on her, and her only, with such intensity that for a moment she felt nervous.

But there was no immediate danger. He would never be able to catch her alone, because she had Ármann beside her. He had always been there, right from the very beginning.

Daníel

He stood there, the words slowly sinking in, feeling as if time were standing still.

He had almost gone the same way as Víkingur.

He'd come so close.

It was by a lucky fluke that he was standing here now, alive.

And there stood Helena too, as coolly as if nothing had happened.

He had seen her fall and hurt herself. She hadn't been able to walk, she'd said. That had been a lie.

Had anyone been telling him the truth, apart from Gunnlaugur? Come to think of it, even Gunnlaugur had shown a disturbingly different side to himself.

It was then that Daníel's gaze dropped to the floor, and he gasped again, his eyes widening in shock.

The stranger who had been sitting in the corner was now sprawled on the floor. It looked as if he was bleeding to death, if he wasn't already dead.

The sight was horrifyingly real, yet so incongruous. What on earth had happened here last night?

'Is he . . . ?'

Daníel scanned their faces, first Ármann's, then Helena's, but he couldn't see Gunnlaugur's as he had his back to him.

Ármann nodded. 'There was a bit of an accident,' he said, his voice so matter-of-fact and emotionless that it made Daníel's blood run cold. For a moment he was afraid he himself might be in danger. But there was nowhere else he could go.

'A bit of an accident . . . ?' Daníel repeated incredulously. 'Did you shoot him?' He peered around the hut again and this time spotted the gun lying on the floor. 'Why did you shoot him? What have I just walked into?'

'I didn't shoot him,' Ármann replied, in the same cold, emotionless voice.

'Oh, then who did? You're not trying to tell me he shot himself?'

'Your mate Gunnlaugur decided to kill the poor bloke. It's a good thing you're here. Maybe you can come up with some ideas, because it's got us stumped.'

Daníel was temporarily lost for words.

'Well, Daníel?' Ármann persisted. 'What do you suggest?'

'What do I suggest? I'm still trying to work out what the fuck is going on . . . Is he dead?'

'It looks like it.'

Daníel seized Gunnlaugur by the shoulder and his friend slowly turned. He was so ashen that Daníel was momentarily taken aback. Gunnlaugur looked as if he had aged ten years overnight.

'Gunnlaugur, what happened?'

'It's quite true,' he said, his voice quiet, faltering, alien. 'I shot him.'

'But why?' Daníel tried with difficulty to stay calm. The atmosphere in there was charged enough already.

'It just happened, Daníel. I was holding the gun and . . . he . . .'

'Did he attack you?'

'No, or – I thought he was going to, you see? He stood up and . . . I just thought he was going to kill us.' Gunnlaugur's voice was thick with horror. 'Honestly, that's what I thought. That he was going to . . .'

'Who is he? I mean, who was he?' Daníel asked, scrutinizing their faces in turn.

'Haven't a clue,' Ármann replied with a shrug. 'Ask your mate here. Maybe they knew each other, seeing as he killed him.'

As far-fetched as this sounded, it occurred to Daníel for a moment that it might be true. There might have been some connection between the stranger and Gunnlaugur that had prompted him to seize the opportunity to get rid of him . . .

No, this was pure paranoia. Of course he would stand by his friend, even though Gunnlaugur hadn't always made this easy for him over the years. Daníel had heard rumours about the rape. And now Gunnlaugur had accidentally shot a complete stranger.

'We can't get hold of anyone from here,' Daníel said,

'but the weather's clearing up. Shouldn't we just head back? Call the police as soon as we get a signal?' When he reached the hut, exhausted after his night's ordeal, he would never have believed he could walk another step. But shock had temporarily driven the tiredness from his mind.

Gunnlaugur lowered his head and didn't respond.

Daníel turned to Helena, but her face was impassive. She had some explaining to do on her own account, he thought.

It was Ármann who replied: 'Well, that's the best option if you really want Gunnlaugur to lose everything – his reputation, his job – and to be condemned as a murderer. How about it? Shall we cast a vote on Gunnlaugur's fate?'

Ármann

He didn't mean it, but Daníel wasn't to know that.

All the same, he was worried that Daníel would figure things out. Ármann had caught the look he had given Helena. And Daníel might prove a tough customer to deal with.

'Cast a vote?' Daníel echoed. 'How do you mean?'

'We came up with some other possible solutions, though we're not happy with any of them.'

'Solutions?'

'To try and save Gunnlaugur's skin. Or maybe you don't want to help get your friend out of this mess?'

'Mess? Are you joking? This isn't a fucking "mess". He's killed someone.'

'Yes,' Ármann said flatly.

'What did you have in mind?'

'We were just discussing that when you came in. One way would be to set fire to the hut, if we had enough fuel. But I don't know if that would work, and of course it would lead to a police inquiry. A better idea would be to . . .'

Gunnlaugur finished the sentence: '. . . make him disappear.'

'Who?' Daníel asked. 'The poor bastard you shot?'

'Yes, I didn't mean . . .'

'We just need to get rid of the body,' Ármann said. 'That should be doable. Then Gunnlaugur can go back to work on Monday morning as if nothing has happened. I can live with it. I didn't know the guy and didn't do anything to him myself. And it won't make my life any better to see Gunnlaugur in jail.'

At this point Helena chipped in, speaking for the first time in a while: 'I'm not so sure about that myself. The truth is, he belongs behind bars.'

Gunnlaugur

To get rid of the body.

Gunnlaugur was finding it almost impossible to reconnect with reality. He would never have believed that he would one day take part in a conversation like this, let alone that he himself would be the guilty party.

He didn't know how or why but Ármann and Helena had decided to stand by him, and now Daníel had joined them, just as Helena seemed to be changing her mind. Thank God he had a true ally in Daníel.

At first, Gunnlaugur had vacillated, feeling that he ought to shoulder the responsibility, but now he had made up his mind to get away with it if he could. He simply couldn't face the shame that would be associated with a prosecution, or a possible spell in prison. The thought alone was horrifying. He had never been able to cope with enclosed spaces, so the idea of being deprived of his freedom and shut up within four walls filled him with a suffocating despair.

'Daníel, you know I don't belong in prison, don't you?'

he appealed to his friend, trying to hide the raw desperation in his voice. 'We'll sort it out, you and me and Ármann, whatever Helena says . . .'

But Daníel didn't reply.

'Won't we, Daníel?'

'I don't know what happened here while I was away,' Daníel began, slowly. 'And I'm not sure I want to know either . . .'

'There's nothing to know . . . It was just an accident . . .'

Daníel didn't seem to be listening. He carried on with what he had been saying: 'But I do know that I don't want to be part of it. I'm just going to head home, as soon as I can get out of here.'

'What do you mean, Daníel?' Gunnlaugur asked, a note of hysteria entering his voice.

'I mean that now it's every man for himself. Sometimes that's just the way it is. Helena sent me out alone in the storm to find a hut that may not even exist, for all I know. It's only by some miracle that I managed to survive. So no way am I going to be suckered into helping anyone get away with murder.'

'It wasn't murder, Daníel, you know that . . .'

'I have no idea whether it was or not.'

'Just what are you suggesting, then?' Ármann asked, rounding on Daníel, and it was evident now that he was angry.

'I don't have to suggest anything. It's got nothing to do with me. And don't you lot imagine for one minute that I'm going to help you burn down the hut or bury the body.'

'There's no way of burying –' Gunnlaugur began, but Ármann cut him short.

'Just shut up, will you, Gunnlaugur?' Ármann looked back at Daníel: 'You're seriously not going to help your friend? Are you happy to send him to prison? For sixteen years? Don't you give a shit about him?'

Gunnlaugur felt as if his neck was in a noose and Daníel was slowly, inexorably, drawing it tight.

'Of course I give a shit, but I'm not going to break the law for him. Or for anyone else, for that matter. Anyway, I don't know if that would really be helping him. Gunnlaugur wouldn't be able to live with what he's done. Sooner or later he'd hand himself in and then he'd have to answer for hiding the body too. And even if he did manage to live with his conscience, crimes like this always get found out in the end . . .'

'That's true,' Helena chimed in unexpectedly. 'Everything comes out in the end. No one can hide a crime like that for ever – murder, I mean.' And Gunnlaugur noticed that her eyes were fixed on Daníel as she uttered the words.

Helena

Daniel didn't respond.

But then she hadn't been expecting him to.

He was a coward, just like his friend. Or ex-friend, rather, as his relationship with Gunnlaugur was unlikely to last out the day.

'It'll all come out in the end,' she repeated, trying to provoke a response.

'May I remind you that I was more dead than alive myself just now,' Daniel said eventually. 'You've got some nerve preaching at me.'

'So what are you planning to do, Daniel? Since you don't want to help us . . .'

'I don't see why I should.'

'If you're not going to help us, what then?'

'What do you mean?'

'Are you going to try and stop us? Or rat on your friend to the police?'

'Helena, for fuck's sake, I haven't thought that far yet, OK? Give me a break. I've just got back into shelter after a hell of a night. I'm frozen half to death, and I can hardly think straight. This mess has nothing to do with me, that's the point. And I don't know if I'd set the police on Gunnlaugur, but I'm not going to lie for you, if that's what you're asking. An innocent man is lying dead on the floor and I don't know why. Does that seem like a normal state of affairs to you? Tell me you weren't seriously intending to set fire to the hut and burn the evidence? Do you really think no one's looking for this man?'

Helena raised her voice, almost screaming now: 'For Christ's sake, Daníel! Does playing with your friends' lives like this seem OK to you? What if you were in this position?'

'I have no intention of going to prison for Gunnlaugur's sake, and that's final. I haven't done anything wrong apart from come on this bloody trip. Which was a terrible mistake. And I don't understand why you two should suddenly care so much about Gunnlaugur . . . Something doesn't add up here. Are you trying to take me for a fool? Besides, Helena, you still owe me an explanation for what happened last night.'

'At least shut the door, Daníel,' Ármann intervened, perhaps in an attempt to defuse the situation. 'I'm freezing.'

Daníel nodded curtly, stepped out of the way and pushed the door shut behind him.

There they were again, the four friends, and the stranger who Gunnlaugur had murdered. The situation could hardly be worse and yet Helena had a powerful premonition that this was only the beginning of their troubles . . .

Daníel

He realized he would have a job withstanding the pressure from Ármann and Helena, who wouldn't give up so easily, but he was less worried about Gunnlaugur, although there was more at stake for him.

The fact puzzled him. Why did Gunnlaugur's fate suddenly matter so much to the others? And why had Helena lied about spraining or breaking her ankle? He had noticed that she wasn't limping now. And there was no way she could have walked back to the hut if she had been as badly injured as she had claimed. Why had she tried to dispatch him to his death?

'We have to stick together now, Daníel. There's no alternative,' Ármann said, his voice steady, but he couldn't disguise the false note.

One step at a time, Daníel thought to himself.

'Helena owes me an explanation first, then we can talk about Gunnlaugur.'

'We don't have an unlimited amount of time. It's getting light out there and . . .'

'Helena, why did you lie to me?' Daníel studied her face, expecting her to go on lying and denying that she had faked her injury.

'Would it have been so terrible, to die like that?' she asked instead.

'What do you mean?'

'Like Víkingur.' Again, she brought up his name, and Daníel shivered.

He had so often pictured the scene when Víkingur's lifeless body was discovered on the mountain road. The image haunted him both in his sleep and in his waking hours.

He remembered him, that last day, remembered his high spirits, how cheerful he'd been, as always, regardless of any friction and bad feeling. Healthy, strong – seemingly indomitable. It would never have occurred to Daníel that the elements would get the better of him. Somehow he had been confident that Víkingur would make it safely back to town and shelter.

But then the unthinkable had happened: Víkingur had died of exposure. And Helena had never got over it, that was clear. She no longer wore her sorrow on her sleeve as she had in the early days after his death, but there was no question that the blow had been more than she could bear.

Yet she had never before referred to the subject as directly with Daníel as she had just now . . .

'With all due respect, I don't understand what Víkingur has to do with this,' he replied. 'What happened to him was a terrible tragedy, but thank God there wasn't a repetition of that last night.' After a pause he added: 'In my case, I mean. Of course, not . . .' He jerked his head at the man on the floor.

'We *are* going to talk about Víkingur. He's dead. You're not. We're going to talk –'

'Helena.' Ármann interrupted. 'This isn't the time or place . . .'

'It's *exactly* the time and place,' she retorted sharply. Then she glared at Daníel again: 'When did you last see Víkingur?'

'What?' He could hardly believe what he was hearing.

'When, Daníel? When? It's a simple enough question.'

'What does it matter? I don't know if I remember –'

'Of course you remember the last time you saw your best friend. You must remember. I'm sure we've . . .'

After a brief pause, Daníel said: 'The day before he disappeared. We were round at my place until quite late, but I can't see what that's got to do with anything. Why are we even talking about him?'

'Because he died.'

Ármann

Why did she have to bring up Víkingur?

Of course, Ármann should have expected it, in the circumstances, given the strain they were under. And given that they were totally screwed, anyway.

Perhaps she felt she had nothing to lose; that anything they let slip now, in that hut, would have no repercussions once they returned to the outside world.

But he had to bite back his irritation. He wasn't angry with her. He had never been angry with Helena.

'I know he died,' Daníel said. 'And I know it was a tragedy, but right now we're trying to . . . well, I don't actually know . . .'

'We're going to talk about Víkingur,' Helena said stubbornly.

Ármann wanted to interrupt, but he knew there was no stopping Helena now.

'Then talk about Víkingur!' Daníel snarled. 'He was no saint or angel, even if you thought he was. He had a temper and he was difficult, though we loved him.'

'You met him the evening before he died?'

'Yes, that's what I just said.'

'And never again after that?'

Ármann concentrated hard and caught that infinitesimal pause because he was listening out for it. He was sure Helena did too.

'Of course not. No one met him after that. He went into the mountains and got lost. I sometimes feel as if you're just looking for someone to blame for what happened. But you can't always find a scapegoat.'

'I don't believe he was alone up there, Daníel.'

Ármann could feel the battle lines being drawn up, the temperature in the hut rising again. Even Gunnlaugur seemed to sense the undercurrents, though he had appeared almost catatonic up to now.

Daníel replied angrily: 'What the hell does Víkingur have to do with the situation we're in now? And why did you lie to me, Helena? I don't understand what's going on, unless . . .'

Ármann glanced at Helena.

'Why did you drag us out here?' Daníel demanded. 'What were you planning to do with us? With . . . me?'

A theory was evidently beginning to form in Daníel's mind. It was clear from the expressions crossing his face, from his choice of words.

'That's it. We're going straight back to town,' Daníel said flatly. Once he'd set his mind on something, it had always been difficult to get him to change it, as Ármann knew from experience. 'We're going to the police, OK? I don't know what's happening here but there's no way in hell I'm helping you with a cover-up. We need to find out who this man was.'

It was as if all the weight of the world had descended on Ármann's shoulders. He could feel the tension building up and up until it became unbearable; he could hear the blood throbbing in his ears. Bracing himself, he watched Daníel with narrowed eyes, then leapt into action the instant Daníel dropped his gaze to the man lying on the floor, the man who was the source of all their trouble.

'Why couldn't you just die?' Ármann roared.

Daníel

He was totally unprepared.

He had stuck to his guns, no doubt to the anger and frustration of his former friends, and of course there was a huge amount at stake – for Gunnlaugur, at least. Yet Gunnlaugur had hung back. More than anything, Daníel was desperate to go home, prey now to the dawning suspicion that he had been dragged out here to the lonely wilderness like a lamb to slaughter.

Daníel's head had been turned away, his attention on the lifeless man on the floor, when Ármann charged him.

He was taken completely by surprise.

Ármann may have had a chequered past, perhaps more than they knew, but he had never used violence against his friends before, or shown even the slightest tendency in that direction.

Daníel went crashing to the floor with a yell and narrowly avoided hitting his head, managing somehow to protect it.

Ármann was strong, no question; he had the advantage

over Daníel in terms of sheer muscle power, and Daníel was hit by the sickening thought that Ármann hadn't just attacked him in the heat of the moment, as a warning to toe the line, but that he had another, more sinister purpose. That Ármann actually meant to do him harm. The first blow was heavy, to put it mildly, and although Daníel had got his arm up in time to prevent it from being any worse, the pain was still shocking.

He found himself wondering why Helena didn't intervene. She had always succeeded in holding Ármann in check and restraining his worst side, but now Daníel had the horrible feeling that she was going to stand by and watch.

He couldn't expect any help from Gunnlaugur either. After all, Daníel had made it abundantly clear that he wasn't going to lie for his old friend's sake, so it would probably suit Gunnlaugur to have him out of the way. Then the three of them could get away with doing whatever they wanted . . .

Daníel had rarely got into fights, and certainly never been involved in anything serious, but he knew it was a different story with Ármann. Sometimes he had wondered how deeply sunk in vice Ármann had been during his addict days, how active he had been in the criminal underworld . . . Had he administered beatings? Had he . . . Could he even have killed someone?

Here he was, coming in again to finish the job.

Summoning every remaining ounce of his strength, Daníel kicked out wildly, and to his surprise the blow found its mark. Ármann groaned aloud and rocked on his feet.

Could Ármann have murdered someone back in his Copenhagen days?

At that moment Daníel believed Ármann capable of pretty much anything. Perhaps he had always known, subconsciously, but had just appreciated having him on his side in case anything ever happened.

Again, the thought struck Daníel that Ármann might have been responsible for the death in the hut but that he had somehow conned Gunnlaugur into taking the blame . . .

Daníel seized the chance to sit up a little while Ármann was recovering his balance and now he noticed in the grey light from the window that blood was pouring from Ármann's nose. Perhaps he'd managed to break it with his kick.

Seeing the fury and hatred in his old friend's eyes, Daníel knew this wasn't over. His mind racing, he ran through his options. He wouldn't be able to make a run for it as the door was shut and outside nothing awaited him but an empty wilderness of snow. Exhausted as he was, he would never be able to get far, even if he knew which direction to go in. He would just have to try to hold his own and pray that one of the others would belatedly intervene to stop this madness, because he knew he would never be able to get the better of Ármann without help.

Time seemed to slow down, the seconds dragging by as slowly as minutes. Daníel had risen to a crouching position and put out a hand to steady himself against the wall. Ármann stared at him, then took a step backwards, as if to get a longer run up to finish the job. Daníel felt his fear intensifying. He was afraid this was it: he was going to die. Death felt closer now than it ever had before, the threat even more viscerally real than when he had been out there, lost in the brutal cold and darkness last night. He expected Ármann's next blow to be the last thing he'd ever feel.

And he wanted to cry: *Are you two really going to stand by and do nothing?*

But there was no point; he couldn't afford to waste his breath on shouting and would probably barely have time to open his mouth before Ármann's next blow fell.

He knew no one was coming to save him.

He and Ármann might as well have been alone in that godforsaken hovel, on that disastrous hunting trip. How the hell had he ever let himself be fooled into coming here?

It had been Ármann who had come up with the idea and planned every last detail.

Was it possible that nothing had happened by chance after all? How much had Ármann prepared and at what point had fate taken over?

Had they always meant it to end this way?

Daníel felt his muscles tensing and realized that if he used his position to launch himself at his opponent, he would have an outside chance of levelling the game.

The image of his girlfriend in London flashed into his mind. He'd thought about her a lot during his night in the snow. Although they hadn't been together that long, somehow they worked as a couple and he missed her.

His previous relationship had ended badly, with a screaming match in the middle of the night after which he had literally thrown his girlfriend out onto the street. He had a tendency to do that – to let his temper get the better of him. Unsurprisingly, she had never forgiven him, although he had regretted it the next morning.

This time he meant to make more of an effort. He was really into the girl he was with and longed to see her again.

It was now or never. He gathered himself and sprang.

Ármann

It hadn't been his intention to hit Daníel such a vicious blow, but it was necessary to teach him a lesson and get him to wake up to the gravity of the situation. There was far too much at stake. After his early mistakes in life, Ármann had found his feet, and more; he'd built up a little business empire in a short time and had vowed to himself that he would never get into trouble with the police again. Now that vow was hanging by a thread, all thanks to Gunnlaugur – and then Daníel had come along, threatening to make things even worse.

Ármann had called on his old tricks from his Copenhagen days, hitting hard and fast, and knew that he hadn't been careful enough. The truth was he didn't really give a damn about the consequences. If Daníel didn't get up again, all it would mean was that they had two bodies on their hands instead of one. Same problem, just a bit bigger.

Look at Daníel, cowering there on the floor, as if he'd given up.

Ármann took a step backwards, then another, wondering if he should leave it at that, but in his heart of hearts he knew that Daníel had one more blow coming to him. Ármann's own nose was bleeding from Daníel's kick and the fight wasn't going to end until they had both drawn blood.

His anger was always so close to the surface, but he had learned to control it, for the most part, since starting up his travel company. He'd always been able to turn to Helena for advice, though she wasn't exactly whiter than white herself. She was just better at hiding her flaws.

He felt his insides churning with a bitter rage against Daníel.

Daníel meant to destroy everything . . .

He could feel his body making the decision for him, gathering itself, prepared to use all its strength to make Daníel suffer.

Gunnlaugur

He shrank back from the fight, closer to Helena.

But he was careful not to go too near her after the incident on Friday night. He had been so afraid that his little miscalculation might have serious repercussions. How laughable those worries seemed now that he was standing in this wretched hut, having murdered a man in cold blood, watching his friends engaged in what looked like a fight to the death.

He felt as if he had stumbled into a hole at the beginning of this trip and was still plummeting headlong into a bottomless abyss.

Everything was over, he thought, and nothing could save him from hitting rock bottom. He would never survive the fall.

So he saw no reason to intervene in the fight. Of course, he should have tried to step between them and help Daníel, but the truth was that he was frightened: he didn't want to get into a struggle with Ármann, as he knew he was no match for him. In addition, part of him felt that

Daníel deserved it. He tried to push the uncomfortable thought away but revenge was sweet, and moments ago Daníel had been refusing to throw him a lifeline, refusing to come to the aid of his old friend. Well, now they were quits. Yet Gunnlaugur was still afraid for Daníel.

There was simply nothing he could do to save him.

Helena

She had to admit to herself that she was enjoying this.

Daníel was only getting what he deserved. That first blow, hard and well aimed. She watched, feeling a deep sense of satisfaction flooding her body, as if she were taking part in the fight herself.

But it came as something of a surprise when, instead of being knocked out by that first punch, Daníel had actually managed to kick Ármann in the face. It had been a feeble riposte, though, that was never going to do any real damage. Like a kitten fighting a lion. Now he was huddled up on the floor, all the wind knocked out of him, as if just waiting for the next blow, and it was impossible to guess whether Ármann would restrain himself now that he was presented with such an easy target. He'd always had a ruthless streak – they both had. A character trait that had served him well in business, once he had finally learned to channel it. Which is why this mustn't end the way Daníel wanted it to. Ármann had put too much effort into building up his company, and himself as well. She couldn't give a damn what happened to Gunn-laugur but she had to look after Ármann.

Her thoughts went homing to Víkingur.

It was his day, the anniversary of his death. She and Ármann hadn't mentioned this once and Gunnlaugur probably didn't have a clue, but Daníel must have figured it out. The day his friend died. Unless he was so utterly cold and devoid of emotion that he hadn't even given it a thought. She had sometimes witnessed that side of him, at college and later; that self-centredness, yet somehow it hadn't held him back at all. He had sailed through life.

Ármann was poised motionless, contemplating his prey, as if delaying purely in order to instil fear and torment his victim a little longer. And she was glad; grateful for the chance to savour this moment.

She stole a glance at Daníel, but if she had expected to see abject terror driving all the other emotions from his face, she was disappointed. He didn't appear frightened in the least. His expression was so unfathomable and strange that she was clutched by a sudden sense of dread. Her gaze swung back to Ármann but he didn't seem to have noticed anything.

And then it happened. Daníel sprang up with such force that she had never seen the like, as if he'd kicked off with his feet as well as his hands. He seemed to fly through the air at Ármann, sending him crashing to the floor.

Only then did Helena finally react.

She leapt into action, trying to dive between them to force them apart, but although the space was small, she was too late. Ármann was on the floor with Daníel on top of him.

Helena shoved weakly at Daníel, trying to push him off, but it proved much easier than she had expected. Instead of resisting, he yielded, moving aside of his own accord. This puzzled her but she was relieved not to have to fight him. That hadn't been the intention; her only thought had been to help Ármann.

Belatedly she registered that something was wrong.

It was like being transported five years back in time. The feeling that gripped her was the same as she had experienced when she learned of Víkingur's death. She felt suddenly ice cold but the coldness was quite different from the chill caused by the unheated hut; much, much deeper and more terrifying, reaching all the way into the deepest recesses of her soul – because Ármann wasn't moving. Blood was pumping from his head, and the pool, so incongruously dark red in the pale morning light, was alarmingly large given how short a time had passed since he hit the floor. Again, she was aware that her sense of time was slipping from her grasp. However hard she tried to be in control of her surroundings at any given moment, time always played tricks on her.

She opened her mouth and screamed.

Daníel

It was Helena's scream that alerted Daníel to what he had done.

It had taken him a moment or two to realize that his attack had succeeded. He had been so desperate, so sure it was futile, but conscious that he had to try; that his only chance of getting out of this alive was to catch Ármann unawares.

Now Ármann was lying on the floor and Daníel was aware of a strange sense of peace. The pain of Ármann's punch to his head had dissipated as soon as the other man fell. Yet the whole thing had taken no more than a few seconds.

The silence following Helena's scream was like the silence of death.

There was no sign, at first glance, that Ármann's head had struck any obstacle on the way down, not until the back of his skull had made contact with the floor. But he wasn't moving.

It dawned on Daníel that perhaps this was what it felt like to kill.

Maybe he had transgressed once before, but then the circumstances had been quite different. This time he felt detached, as if it wasn't happening to him, and there was no sense of guilt. After all, he hadn't done anything wrong.

That was the main thing, now as it was then.

He hadn't done anything wrong at all.

This time he had been under attack: Ármann had wanted to kill him, it was as simple as that, and Daníel had had no choice but to defend himself. He'd known that he might not survive Ármann's next onslaught – his life would have been in danger – but now that the dust had settled, Daníel was the one left standing. Not as victor – he couldn't think of it like that – but alive. And what more could anyone ask?

He threw a sideways glance at Helena and she reacted by shoving him violently away.

'You've killed him, Daníel. You've killed . . .'

Daníel rocked but kept his balance, then he shifted back, as far out of reach as he could get, almost into the corner.

'It was his fault,' he protested. He hadn't actually meant to say it aloud but he'd felt he had to justify his own action. And he still had unfinished business with Helena.

'It wasn't his fault, Daníel!' She was shrieking now. 'It was your fault. You killed him. You killed my brother!'

Gunnlaugur

They had never been particularly alike in appearance and few people would have guessed they were brother and sister, let alone that they were twins.

Yet there was a sense in which they were almost the mirror image of each other, except that one had a touch more darkness in their soul. Originally, Gunnlaugur had been under the impression that this was Ármann, but as the years passed by it had become increasingly plain that it was Helena who controlled her brother, not the other way round.

Her brother who was now lying on the floor, apparently dead.

Two bodies.

And this time Daníel was responsible.

The thought filled Gunnlaugur with an inexplicable sense of relief, as if his own crime had been rendered less serious now that another man had been killed. Of course, this wasn't logical, but he couldn't help feeling a little better than he had before. And pleased too that Daníel would have to go through the same ordeal as him. The shame, the guilt, the endless downward spiral of negative emotions.

Now Daníel would become an outcast too; he would lose his friends, his job, his girlfriend. At least he had a girlfriend to lose. Gunnlaugur felt a sudden flare of envy, despite the bizarre situation. Perhaps these were feelings that had always been there, seething under the surface, and had only now burst forth. Daníel was the handsome, talented guy who everybody liked, best friend of Víkingur and Ármann, while Gunnlaugur had lurked on the sidelines, calling Daníel his best friend because he didn't have anyone else. If Helena hadn't been head over heels in love with Víkingur, Daníel would probably have had a chance with her too. But now Daníel would be sharing the same fate as Gunnlaugur; he had no guardian angel to protect him any more.

'He attacked me,' Daníel said to Helena in a tightly controlled voice. 'You were watching. You were both watching. He was going to kill me. You don't even need to threaten me – I'm going straight to the police myself. This is totally fucked up. I've literally had to fight for my life, not once but twice. First out in the snow, then in a fight with someone who was supposed to be my friend.'

Gunnlaugur's head began to spin as he took in what Daníel was saying.

So they weren't in this together after all?

Yet again he experienced a burning sense of grievance. Life was so unfair: Daníel had been dealt a handful of aces, while Gunnlaugur had been stuck with nothing but losing cards.

'You killed him, Daníel,' he protested, though it would probably have been wiser for him to keep his mouth shut and leave Helena and Daníel to fight it out.

Daníel smiled coldly. 'You killed that man last night. Don't try to pretend it's the same.'

Gunnlaugur had no answer to that. He was silent, trying to picture how things would play out now. There was no longer anything to prevent him from being forced to stand trial. And of course Daníel was right: the two incidents were scarcely comparable. Gunnlaugur had shot a man in cold blood, whereas Daníel had been fighting for his life.

Gunnlaugur had no more arguments. It was over.

Helena

She shouldn't have given in to her feelings by shoving Daníel like that. She had to control her rage. Freaking out wouldn't achieve anything. Yes, she had lost her brother – who was also her best friend. And the person responsible for taking him away was Daníel, the man who had already destroyed her life once before. But she needed to plot her next moves carefully.

'You're both going to prison,' she said, trying to keep her voice steady. 'But I'll help you get back to town; I should be able to find the way back to the lodge. Then we'll need to get someone out here to fetch the bodies. I'm not leaving Ármann lying here any longer than necessary.'

She glanced at Gunnlaugur: his face was blank. It was Daníel who gave her more cause for concern.

He wore a look of intense concentration that alarmed her.

'Come on.' She moved towards the door. Gunnlaugur stepped out of her way as if nothing could be more natural. 'There's no time to lose,' she added.

She opened the door, to be hit by a wall of cold air, but at least the wind had dropped at last. Before her, an undulating white landscape spread out as far as the eye could see under a leaden sky. She threw a look over her shoulder.

Daníel hadn't stirred. 'We need to talk first,' he said. 'Talk about Víkingur, remember?'

'What about him?'

'This is the anniversary of his death. Did you think I hadn't realized?'

She was silent.

'He died of exposure. And I almost went the same way last night.'

Still she didn't speak. She wanted to know what he was going to say.

'It was no coincidence. That was all I could think about as I was struggling to get back to the hut, in between praying that I'd find it again. I kept thinking that it couldn't be a coincidence. And I remembered, Helena . . .'

He was staring at her, his cold eyes boring into her.

'I remembered that it was you who dragged me out into the storm and led me into the unknown, pretending to show me the way. And the same suspicion kept sneaking into my mind: were you trying to lead me to my death? I couldn't believe it, though, Helena – you know why? Because you yourself were in trouble. You'd injured your ankle, which meant we were both in the same boat.'

'Yes, Helena was limping when she got back here,' Gunnlaugur chipped in, then immediately seemed to regret his interruption.

'Really? I doubt it. She's certainly staged a quick recovery.' Daníel turned that inquisitorial gaze back on her: 'You don't seem very badly injured, Helena, do you? You're not fooling anyone, you know. There's no point keeping up the pretence now I've seen through you.'

He was right: she might as well drop the act.

'I know it was your fault, Daníel,' she said quietly but firmly. 'I know you killed Víkingur.'

'What!? That's total bullshit. Of course I didn't kill Víkingur.'

To give him his due, he made it sound convincing.

'Let's cut the crap, Daníel. It's time to tell the truth.'

And then Gunnlaugur seemed suddenly to come to life, blurting out: 'Nobody knows he was here.'

Helena paused and blinked at him: 'What?'

'That's what Ármann said. I just remembered.'

'What did he say?' Daníel asked.

'That nobody knew that man was here, the . . .' Gunnlaugur trailed off.

'How could Ármann have known that?' Daníel asked, his voice as sharp as the look he now directed at Helena.

'We might as well lay our cards on the table,' Helena said. 'It's time the truth came out about a number of things. Including why this man – this stranger – is lying dead on the floor.'

Daníel

Daníel stared at her incredulously.

Again, he felt a frisson of fear run through him. There was such a sinister, unnatural air of calm about her.

In this moment he was almost more frightened of her than he had been of her brother.

In his confusion, he wondered if she was asking him about the stranger, as though she thought he might know of some reason for the man's presence in the hut.

'Do you know something about him?' Daníel asked her, warily.

'It doesn't matter any more,' she said. 'It wasn't my idea, anyway.'

As she said it, Daníel felt a strong conviction that this last part was a total lie. 'What wasn't your idea?'

'To bring that man into it.'

Daníel drew in a sharp breath. Had the stranger in the corner been here by some machination of the twins? 'Did he come with you?' he asked.

'Tell me about Víkingur,' she countered.

'Sorry?'

'About the day Víkingur died.'

'We've already been over this, Helena. I saw him the night before.'

'And then you both went out of town together. I know. A few months ago I met a witness who saw you both. You stopped at a petrol station.'

Daníel felt as if all the oxygen had been sucked out of the air in the hut.

Helena pressed on, inexorably: 'And I know you had the day off. I checked, asked around. You were appearing in a play at the theatre, but there was no performance that evening. And . . .'

Daníel stood there, rigid with shock, trying to block out the sound of her words. Because he didn't want to hear what she had to say. He couldn't bear it.

Helena

She had read up on the subject repeatedly, far more often than was healthy, only to regret it every time.

As a result she knew too much and couldn't wipe any of the details from her mind.

She believed she knew exactly how Víkingur had died, almost as if she had been there, suffering with him, though in reality she had been far from his side.

She hadn't been there to save him and she brooded on the fact every day. Could she have done something? If she had only known where he was going, if she had only been with him . . . Sometimes she felt as if it were her fault, though of course that was absurd.

It had been bitterly cold that night, obviously. Winter nights in Iceland were invariably cold.

And he had been freezing. That went without saying. She could imagine the fits of shivering that would have seized him as the icy temperature crept into his flesh. His blood vessels would have contracted, though no doubt Víkingur had done his damnedest to keep moving to warm himself up, refusing to believe that he wouldn't find shelter; refusing to lose hope. Because it hadn't been in Víkingur's nature to give up, and Helena knew he had never abandoned hope that night, though of course the cold had defeated him in the end.

By that stage his shivering would have ceased, according to what she had read.

That had been the hardest part to believe at first, but she had to accept the facts. His body temperature would have gradually sunk and his reactions become increasingly sluggish.

Then his shivering would have stopped. It must have happened like that. She had so often dwelt on that moment. Had he been fooled into thinking that things were improving, that he would make it, after all? That he was warming up again?

If so, he must soon have realized that something was wrong. His blood vessels would have continued to contract, according to the accounts she had read, and gradually his heart would have slowed and his life force ebbed, until it must have filtered into Víkingur's mind that it could only end one way. She wondered how long that realization had lasted, how long he had suffered, knowing that he was dying. After that, the restricted blood flow would have begun to take effect, making him increasingly dizzy and confused, until eventually he lost consciousness. His body temperature would have dropped to 31 or 32 degrees Celsius by the time he went to sleep, in the place where his body had later been found. She knew, or sensed, it. His heartbeat would have grown ever fainter until finally it ceased altogether.

But even then there would still have been hope. The doctor she had spoken to had told her, after she'd questioned him repeatedly, that death wouldn't necessarily have come quickly. The body required less oxygen in intense cold, and occasionally people had been successfully brought back to life, even though their body temperature had dropped that low. Miracles sometimes happened, he had told her.

Just not in Víkingur's case.

Daníel

He would never tell a soul what happened that day.

That's what he had promised himself so often. Of course, he couldn't stop thinking about it, but it was some consolation to know that he would never have to find words to describe the experience. He would never have to confess to his tragic, fatal mistake.

It had been such a glorious day, but Daníel should have known that nature was often at its cruellest when you were most unsuspecting, especially in Iceland. It never gave quarter; you could never be completely secure. Even the brightest summer days could prove hazardous if you didn't take care or show a proper respect for conditions this close to the Arctic Circle. Lulled into a false sense of security by the beautiful winter's day, the two friends – Daníel and Víkingur – had decided on the spur of the moment to head up into the highlands on a little-used mountain road. Because the weather was so fine; because they were young, strong and invincible. In those days, with the arrogance of youth, they had believed themselves immortal. They'd taken Daníel's car; he'd been driving and in charge of the route, and the outing had begun promisingly enough. They hadn't mentioned it to anyone; not out of a deliberate desire for secrecy, it was just that sometimes it was fun to be able to drop off the radar for a while. Although they'd both been busy at work, they'd been discussing various ideas for business opportunities and possible future collaborations. They'd enjoyed each other's company.

Daníel remembered it vividly: the nip in the air, the perfect stillness, the astounding clarity and beauty of a sunny winter's day in Iceland. If you found a place out of the wind it could feel like a fine, if chilly, summer's day. For much of the drive it had been exactly that kind of weather.

They had stopped far from the nearest human habitation, on a track so rough it hardly deserved the name of road and was almost indistinguishable from the rocky ground stretching out on every side. They were alone, with not another soul in sight as far as the eye could see.

A sunny winter's day, as if summer had made an unseasonable return and nature had no dangers lying in wait. It had still been broad daylight when the quarrel broke out. Really, you could hardly even call it a quarrel at first, just a disagreement about something trivial. Daníel partly blamed himself but knew that Víkingur had also been at fault. It was only natural; friends sometimes needed a row to clear the air and reset their relationship, and perhaps the long drive had contributed to making them both irritable.

In other words, there had been nothing remarkable about their falling-out until Víkingur ordered Daníel to stop the car. He had obeyed, with no suspicion of the repercussions his decision was to have. They had carried on shouting at each other. Víkingur had always had a temper, though his bark was worse than his bite. He hated conceding points to anyone else and always wanted to be right.

Then Víkingur had said, out there in the middle of nowhere: *Fine, I'll walk back.* The words were still etched crystal clear in Daníel's memory, so infinitely terrible.

Walk? Are you kidding?

Daníel's reply had been along those lines, though he couldn't remember his exact words as well as he could Víkingur's. Naturally, he'd thought it was a crazy idea. It had been perfectly clear that Víkingur would never be able to make it back on foot. Perhaps he had been expecting to hitch a lift, confident that another car would come driving along this lonely track in the dead of winter, or perhaps he hadn't expected Daníel to take him at his word. Or else he had simply miscalculated, underestimating the distance and the freezing temperatures that would be lying in wait for him as soon as the sun had set.

And Daníel had taken the decision that he had regretted ever since.

He had replayed their conversation over and over again in his head, with variations, the sun always equally bright in his memory, and the end as cruelly inevitable.

Víkingur had opened the passenger door and stormed off, and Daníel had run after him, leaving the car in the middle of the track. There was no risk of an accident, he knew, because there was nothing else moving in the wide, treeless landscape. It should have been obvious to both of them that they were the only ones out there that day, but Víkingur had been so pig-headed at times. They hadn't encountered a single car since they left the Ring Road, many kilometres back.

Daníel had caught up with Víkingur and grabbed him roughly by the shoulder. *What are you thinking of? Where are you going?* And the quarrel had broken out again; they could yell at the top of their lungs since there was no one else to hear. Their words flew into the void, into the wastes, and vanished, and the same must have been true of Víkingur's cry of despair when he found himself alone – or so Daníel imagined. At times his imagination was so unforgivingly bleak.

Daníel had tried in vain to talk his friend round.

Just go. I don't need you, Víkingur had sneered.

It had made Daníel so angry that in the end he had given up, stomped back to the car, got in and driven away. Víkingur had charged off down the track, the way they had come, and Daníel remembered so well the moment when he roared past him, gunning the engine, never throwing him so much as a backward glance.

He also remembered what he had been thinking at the time: *It'll do him good to feel what it's like to be cold.*

The truth was that Víkingur hadn't been warmly enough dressed to hike for hours along a desolate mountain road. When they set out, they'd only talked about going for a gentle stroll in the sun before getting back in the car. But the sun had been so quick to disappear.

Daníel had put his foot down on the way back, feeling the rage coursing through his body. He had pictured Víkingur arriving back in town, frozen, bedraggled and exhausted, having learned his lesson not to be such a difficult, stubborn bastard.

That evening, Daníel had drunk a beer or two before having an early night. His sleep had been plagued by dreams of Víkingur.

It wasn't until the following morning that he began to feel worried. Surely his friend had made it back to town? Gradually it had dawned on Daníel what he'd done. He'd abandoned Víkingur alone in the highlands, utterly helpless – there hadn't even been a mobile phone signal where they'd stopped the car. They'd lost it a long time before that, Daníel belatedly remembered now.

He kept a close eye on his phone but didn't dare to call Víkingur. He had realized that, in the worst-case scenario, he would have to maintain a certain distance from the events. Although he wasn't well versed in the law, he was pretty sure that his behaviour would be judged on a par with manslaughter.

And of course he only made matters worse by failing to alert the police first thing that morning. He didn't even dare go back to the spot himself to search for his friend. There was too big a risk of bumping into a mountain-rescue team or the police and being forced to account for what he was doing there. As it was, no one knew that he and Víkingur had gone for that drive together.

Naturally, the day of the trip was indelibly etched in his memory, but the following day haunted Daníel almost as much. He could still summon up that sense of dread. It had snowed – beautiful, big flakes falling softly out of the sky, a reminder of the true meaning of winter and the merciless elements. He had felt as if he were suffocating. Of course, he'd had an intuition as soon as he awoke that it was too late to save his friend.

The day was wearing on by the time he finally received a phone call, from Helena. She hadn't seen Víkingur and couldn't reach him on his mobile. It had taken every ounce of Daníel's strength to lie to her, claiming he hadn't seen Víkingur since the day before yesterday. And it struck him then that he had crossed a line from which it would be hard to return. He couldn't face having to answer for the fact he'd abandoned his friend in the highlands, miles from the nearest habitation, in the depths of winter. Despite knowing that living with the shame and guilt would be almost harder to bear than any punishment, he was even more afraid of being charged with manslaughter and sent to prison. Helena had been terribly anxious on the phone, referring to the bouts of depression Víkingur suffered from at times. Her boyfriend had vanished and it was plain that she was afraid he might have taken his own life. They searched for Víkingur with the help of the mountain-rescue teams, mainly in the area where he and Helena had lived, but fortunately the search hadn't taken long. That very evening he had been found in the highlands, by the old mountain road. A driver had come across his body, at quite a distance from the spot where their ways had parted, Daníel guessed later. His friend had been trying to walk back to the Ring Road but had collapsed from cold and exhaustion on the way.

Incredible as it seemed, there hadn't been a thorough investigation. Although there was clearly no explanation for how Víkingur had got so far into the highlands without a car, the police had worked on the assumption that his death had been the result of depression. He had made his way out of town somehow, by hitching a lift or catching a bus, then just kept on walking into the wilds until he could go no further. It didn't seem to have crossed anyone's mind that Víkingur might have been walking in the opposite direction, trying to get back to the main road before darkness fell.

So Daníel had got away with it. No one hated him, no one judged him; he didn't have to share what he had done with anyone except himself and his conscience. And somehow he had survived that struggle with his sanity intact. The key was not to let himself brood on it day in, day out, but to think about Víkingur as little as possible and, it went without saying, never tell anybody else what had happened.

The incident probably explained why he had ended up staying so long in London and was so reluctant to move home. He'd wanted to try his luck on the stage there and see if he could get his big break abroad, or at least that was the story he had told his friends, but in his heart of hearts he must have known that he had other reasons. He no longer felt comfortable living in his harsh native land, where he had inadvertently caused the death of his best friend. His trips home were few and far between, and he rarely stayed long, feeling more at ease in London, where he played a different role: the role of the Icelandic actor. His much younger girlfriend had not only never met Víkingur but didn't even know he had ever existed, and Daníel had no plans to introduce her to his Icelandic friends back home.

He had vowed to himself that he would never admit anything about that fateful day; never confess to any wrong-doing. In this, silence was his best friend and refuge.

But now, five years later, up here on the eastern moors, Helena was asking the question he had been dreading every single day since Víkingur died.

'Did you leave him behind, Daníel?'

A simple enough question.

He had rehearsed his answer, probably more often than he liked to admit to himself, practising his expressions, the astonishment and outrage. Yet despite his talents as an actor, this role was taxing his skills to the limit.

'I wasn't with him. He was alone. Come on, Helena, you know that perfectly well.'

He met and held her gaze, and for a moment he had the illusion that all his sins were reflected in her eyes as he trotted out his well-rehearsed reply, like an actor who knew his lines so well that his performance failed to convince. There were only two people in the audience this time: Gunnlaugur was there somewhere in the background and didn't matter, but Helena plainly wasn't fooled.

Helena

There was no shadow of doubt in her mind that Daníel was lying, but it seemed he had no intention of giving way. And despite her conviction that she was right, she knew it would be hard to prove conclusively that Daníel had been there and abandoned his friend.

She had no way of knowing what had passed between them, whether they had fallen out or Daníel had really intended to kill Víkingur. In the end, it didn't matter. All she needed was to trick him into confessing. That was the first step.

It occurred to her that it might be best to carry on talking and attempt to win his trust by keeping no secrets back herself.

'There's no point continuing with this game,' she said. 'I suggest we clear the air.'

He smiled.

How dare he smile?

'I have nothing to hide,' he said, still with that wide-eyed candour. 'I'm going straight back to town and telling the police what happened. Then maybe we'll be able to clear the air. We'll find out who that man was' – he gestured at the body – 'and whether he had any connection to Ármann – or to you . . . And then perhaps we'll get to the bottom of why you tried to kill me, Helena. Why you dragged me out into the dark in the middle of a storm and left me there. It was only by pure chance that I survived, Helena. A lucky fluke.'

'You were supposed to die like Víkingur!' she burst out, against her own better judgement. Sometimes her temper broke free of its restraints, though she generally managed to keep it under control. She had mostly bottled up her worst feelings, discussing them with no one but Ármann, who could be trusted to solve the problem, one way or another. But now that Ármann was no longer here, it was as if the restraining wall had crumbled.

While she was waiting for Daníel's reaction, it occurred to her that maybe she had an ace up her sleeve after all. There would be no way now of disposing of both bodies. The three of them would have to give a full account of what had happened: Gunnlaugur wouldn't be able to avoid prosecution for manslaughter; Daníel would face charges for Ármann's death, however that turned out, and Daníel would similarly accuse her – justly, as it happened, though she would never admit to the fact. She had indeed tried to lure him to his death. Then the police would demand to know who the stranger was, and it would only be a matter of time before the truth emerged.

The whole thing was one enormous fuck-up. Nothing had gone as planned.

On the other hand, they all had something to gain from making the problem disappear.

She could take over the running of Ármann's company – in the shadow of the tragic events, of course, but that wouldn't prevent the business from continuing. She knew she would make a good director. There were serious sums of money at stake too, as the company was extremely valuable and she was the sole heir. Ármann hadn't had any children and their parents were dead.

Gunnlaugur could carry on living his life, though with murder and rape on his conscience.

Daníel, meanwhile, could go home and continue with his existence as if nothing had happened. Presumably he would want to do Gunnlaugur a favour too, by saving him from jail.

'You were supposed to die,' she repeated, because it no longer made any difference. And Daníel's reaction didn't matter either. She had slotted all the pieces of the puzzle into the right places in her mind. There was only one possible outcome: a temporary cessation of hostilities. But it wasn't the end. The day of reckoning was merely postponed.

Gunnlaugur

As the seconds ticked by it became ever more apparent to him that there was no way out. No one was going to rescue him.

Gunnlaugur had been dithering over the question of whether he could take part in the deception and lies to avoid shouldering responsibility for his crimes. It was only now that this possibility had abruptly been closed off that the full horror of his position came home to him.

Then Helena's words penetrated his thoughts, distracting and baffling him.

Had she genuinely meant to kill Daníel or was she just upset that he had survived?

He didn't dare ask her. She scared him to death and he was so ashamed of his unforgivable behaviour on Friday night.

Those two, Helena and Daníel, would work it out between them, one way or another, hopefully without coming to blows, but the outcome would always be the same: Gunnlaugur would be sacrificed. He had occasionally taken on cases defending clients who were accused of breaking the law, some for trivial offences, others for more major ones. And every time he had been grateful to be the one wearing the robe, a neutral representative of the accused. At the end of the working day he could go home – to an empty house, admittedly – but at least home, whereas the accused was left to languish under a nightmarish cloud of uncertainty. Some defendants had to sleep in a prison cell, others were afraid of ending up there in the near future. And now, by an irony of fate, the roles had been rearranged, the cards had been dealt out again, and he had ended up with the worst hand imaginable.

Daniel

'Why, Helena?'

She seemed chillingly calm and composed, given the circumstances, as if she knew something they didn't, which was probably true. He no longer doubted that she held all the cards. The only question was how many secrets she was prepared to share with them.

'Why did you lie to me and send me on a wild goose chase in the snow like that?'

'You must have worked it out, Daniel. You're not stupid.'

He could feel his temper rising. 'So you're not even going to deny it? That you deliberately abandoned me out there in the blizzard?'

'It's too late for lies now, Daniel.'

The patronizing way she kept repeating his name was getting on his nerves.

'But why? Tell me!' Of course, he knew the answer: it was blindingly obvious. But *Never admit anything* was the mantra he meant to stick to until his last breath.

'You know,' she said, as if she'd read his mind. 'Don't pretend you don't understand. It was because of Víkingur, of course. You abandoned him and I abandoned you. There's a certain justice in that, don't you think? You can't take it too badly, Daníel.'

'Not take it too badly? Is this some kind of joke?'

'Sometimes that's how justice works, Daníel. Sometimes we have to help it along. You need to take responsibility for what you've done.'

'But I didn't do anything! Not a bloody thing!' he yelled, impressing himself with how convincing it sounded.

A smile touched Helena's lips. She seemed amused by the game, and once again he had the deeply uncomfortable sense that she had won. But he couldn't for the life of him work out how.

'What . . . ? Just let me try to get my head around this,' he said, making an effort to stay calm. He couldn't afford to lose his temper again. 'Did you bring me here, on this hunting trip, with the express intention of killing me?'

She didn't answer.

'Did you predict the storm? Better than the Met Office, perhaps?'

She merely smiled again.

But this time he left his question hanging in the air until eventually she relented.

'The weather, yes.' Another pause for effect. 'That was actually an unexpected bonus, as well as being a bit of a pain.'

'What? How do you mean?'

'We weren't expecting a storm.'

'We? You and . . . ?' He glanced inadvertently at Gunn-laugur and felt a sharp pain twisting his stomach. Had all three of them been in it together, colluding in the plot to get rid of him? *You too, Gunnlaugur?*

Gunnlaugur shook his head, though Daníel hadn't accused him of anything. Not aloud. 'Daníel, I haven't a clue what she's talking about. You've got to believe me.'

It appeared that Gunnlaugur still wanted more than anything to be in Daníel's good books, even though only a short time ago Daníel had been ready to betray him.

'Ármann and I, of course,' Helena said, as if nothing could be more natural.

'You plotted this together?' Daníel exclaimed, though he wasn't quite sure exactly what he was referring to. Still, he should have guessed that if Helena had intended to harm him, her brother would have been in on the plan. They had always worked as a team.

'Yes,' she said curtly.

'Then why did you bring Gunnlaugur along?'

'We thought he'd make a useful witness. As a lawyer – maybe not a respected one, but a reliable witness in the eyes of the law. It was such a brilliant plan, Daníel. You were supposed to die. And everything was going smoothly until the weather put a kibosh on things. Then you man-aged to find your way back – who would have believed it? And Gunnlaugur had to go and kill someone. It . . .'

She paused and Daníel held his breath.

'Everything went wrong,' she said, and sighed. From her manner one would have thought she was referring to some trivial game that had gone awry, not attempted murder.

'You can say that again,' Daníel retorted, moving to put a little more distance between them. He wasn't afraid of her, exactly, but her manner was deeply disturbing. What kind of person could be so composed, amused even, when admitting to such things? Especially after seeing her beloved twin brother killed in front of her eyes. 'And don't forget the poor guy who was in the hut when we arrived,' he added. 'The wrong man in the wrong place, was he?'

Helena smiled. 'Well, naturally we'd arranged for him to be here.'

Helena

There was no point trying to cover it up. The police would identify the body. And Ármann had let slip an incriminating comment, as Gunnlaugur had noticed, when he claimed that nobody had known the man was there.

She derived some private amusement from observing the look of disbelief on Daníel's face. Every detail had been carefully planned, perhaps too carefully, she had felt at times, but the ends were supposed to justify the means: to avenge Víkingur's death . . .

'You arranged it?' Daníel echoed, and she noticed an odd glint in his eye, a flash of fear, which gave her intense pleasure.

She was doing her best to ignore what had happened to her brother, to push the devastating event to the back of her mind and focus instead on getting this conversation out of the way. There were immediate problems that needed solving. After that, they could head out into the icy morning and start the long journey home. She mustn't let herself think about Ármann; she must keep her shattering grief at bay and stick to her purpose. There would be a time to mourn him later in private. Probably not by shedding any tears, though. That wasn't her style.

'Yes.'

'So who was he?' This time it wasn't Daníel who asked; Gunnlaugur had forestalled him, and the reason was clear: he wanted to know who he'd killed.

'I don't remember his name, to be honest,' she said. 'Ármann may not even have told me. He was some foreign labourer who was working for Ármann – I think that's all I was told. It doesn't really matter. He was well paid for this little job on the side. Afterwards he was supposed to go back to helping Ármann build a hotel. We assumed he would have left the country before anyone could connect him to this hut. No one would ever find out who he was or what he had been doing here.'

'Hang on. I'm having a hard time following this,' Daníel said. 'You're telling me you paid the man to lie in wait for us? Did you know a storm was on its way?'

'I've already told you, Daníel: the blizzard took us by surprise. It meant we reached the hut early. The storm blew up out of nowhere. We were going to . . .' She hesitated, wondering belatedly if she was saying too much. For an instant she asked herself: *What would Ármann have wanted?* But of course that didn't matter because he no longer had any say; perhaps he'd never really had a say in any of this.

'You were going to what?' Daníel asked sharply.

'We were going to bring you here yesterday evening. The plan was to pretend to lose our way. Not really, of course, because Ármann and I know this area pretty well. And this guy was meant to wait here for us, in the corner, with a gun; just sit there and look threatening . . .' She pointed at the chair. It had been such a good idea of her brother's. Such a brilliant idea . . . 'We were worried he'd be caught out when we got here earlier than expected, but we knew the noise of us breaking open the key box would give him time to put out his torch and get into position.'

'Why did you want him here?' Again it was Daníel who asked.

'To create a menacing atmosphere – you know, because we didn't realize there would be a storm. We were going to arrange it so that you went to fetch help, Daníel. Instead of sending you to the hut with the radio, which would have been too easy to find in good weather, we were going to show you the way, the direct route, "only an hour's walk", to the nearest human habitation. Except not really, you see? In fact, we would send you on the most direct route to an icy death. The weather wouldn't have mattered, because it's easy enough to lose your way on the featureless moors in any conditions. Thanks to us, you would have set off in the wrong direction, heading for the wilderness, walked for an hour, further and further into the highlands, and then it would gradually have dawned on you that you were lost. So, really, Daníel . . .'

She paused again for effect, then went on: 'Really, it would have been the perfect murder.'

Daníel

'You're bullshitting me,' he said.

His so-called friends had led him into a trap with the direct intention of killing him.

Little by little it was sinking in that he had unwittingly been staring death in the face all weekend and had had an incredibly narrow escape. He felt as if the life force had never been stronger within him than at this moment, although he was still standing in the same small room as the person who had tried to murder him.

'I'm not bullshitting you. You must understand that it had to happen, Daníel.'

He had been betrayed. He was angry, but in a way his anger wasn't justified. He knew that. Which was why he had no intention of taking revenge on Helena. All he wanted was to go home. It went without saying that he would never see her again, not if he could avoid it, but at least he felt that now they were quits. Leaving Víkingur behind like that had been a tragic mistake, but perhaps he would be able to sleep a little more easily at night after what had happened here. In some ways it was a relief to know that Helena had found out the truth. He wouldn't have to admit anything; it didn't matter, as she already knew. She had been straight with him and, who knows, perhaps in time they would bury the hatchet. All the things that remained unsaid between them would eventually be understood.

'So what now?'

'Or do you mean, then what? Then . . .' She pointed at Gunnlaugur. 'Then this useless piece of shit had to ruin everything. I didn't want to bring him along but Ármann insisted we had to have a witness to confirm that Daníel had gone out to fetch help, because we didn't know what to do about the menacing man in the hut. Of course, we'd have made sure that no one could trace the man afterwards. By the time the mountain-rescue team reached the hut, he'd have vanished. You would have been dead, Daníel, and we would have been free to carry on with our lives. But, sadly, it didn't work out like that. You survived against all the odds, but there was nothing we could do about that, and Gunnlaugur . . . Gunnlaugur shot the guy. At that point Ármann and I were forced to step in.'

'Why?' Gunnlaugur asked.

'Why?' Helena repeated scornfully. 'Christ, don't you understand anything? Because the police would have identified the body, of course. Not immediately, but sooner or later, and then his link to Ármann would have come out, and . . . obviously, we'd have been screwed. Besides, he wasn't supposed to die! You were the one who was supposed to die.' She was looking at Daníel again, but there was no bitter emphasis in her voice now, no vehemence; she might have been presenting a mundane fact.

'We're in exactly the same position,' Daniel pointed out. It was like a game of chess and suddenly he felt he had the upper hand. 'We'll go back to town and tell the true story. I'm not worried for my own sake, but you're not going to come out of it well.'

'I have a different proposal, Daniel.'

Helena

'Let's call a truce.'

It was hard for her to say those words aloud but she had no choice.

'What?'

Daníel's look of astonishment appeared to be genuine.

'Ármann is the only person who can save us now, and I think he would have wanted that.'

He would have wanted to save her, and her alone, but she wasn't going to tell them that.

She'd earned Daníel and Gunnlaugur's trust, she was sure of it. She had come clean, though of course she hadn't given them any solid evidence; just one person's word against another's.

Her priority now was to escape unscathed from the fallout of this weekend and focus on taking over the reins of Ármann's company. She had a much better head for business than her brother; she'd just never had the break she needed. His success in the travel business had pretty much fallen into his lap – he hadn't earned it. It wasn't that she had envied him exactly, but now that the opportunity had presented itself, she wasn't going to let it slip through her grasp.

'How can Ármann save us?' Daníel asked, his anger flaring up again. 'He tried to kill me and now he's . . . dead.'

Daniel

Although he didn't for a minute trust Helena, he got the feeling that this time she was sincere; perhaps she did want to help him and Gunnlaugur escape from the hell that had been created in this godforsaken hut, if only for her own sake.

He surveyed the bodies lying lifeless on the floor, the horrifying aftermath, as the light of a new day framed the events of the night with brutal clarity. No doubt Helena's main concern was to save her own skin, but then what else could one expect of her?

'We'll leave them behind,' Helena said. She uttered the words with an unsettling air of calm, as if nothing could be more natural. After all these years, Daniel felt that only now had he got the measure of her and learned what kind of person she was underneath.

'Then what?' he asked.

'We'll say they got into a fight. Two friends who worked together; the combination of booze and guns – it was bound to end . . . it did end . . .' There was a moment's silence before she finished: '. . . in tragedy.'

Gunnlaugur said nothing.

Daníel took a little time to reflect before responding. It might just work. If what Helena had said was true, Ármann and the stranger had been acquainted. So the story would go that the five of them had set out on this trip together, only to get lost and end up seeking refuge from the storm in this hut. Then what?

'Of course, we'll have to tamper with some of the evidence,' Helena said coolly, 'but I don't think that'll be too difficult. We split up into two groups for the shoot, didn't we? The three of us in one party and the two of them in another. And we'd planned to rendezvous at the hut before heading back to the lodge. Then the storm threw a spanner in the works. They got to the hut ahead of us, and when we reached it we were met by this horrific sight. Clearly, there had been a fistfight. And shots had been fired on both sides, then somehow Ármann had fallen and hit his head.'

'On both sides?' Gunnlaugur queried, finally finding his voice.

'We'll make it look like that. We'll put the gun in the man's hands and make him shoot once into the wall. Then we'll swap your gun for Ármann's and put his fingerprints on it, so it looks as if he shot the guy. Such a terrible tragedy. We don't know what happened, not exactly, but we heard them arguing about pay and conditions when they were drinking on Friday evening, didn't we? This guy was insisting on being given a share in the company. How does that sound?'

'But you say you don't even know what the guy was called,' Daníel objected. 'How are you going to explain that if you tell the police he was with us all weekend?'

Helena didn't bat an eyelid. 'We'll say Ármann always referred to him by a jokey nickname – don't worry, we'll make something up – and that we never actually heard his real name.'

Daníel was shaken by Helena's demeanour. There was her twin brother, lying dead at her feet, while she coolly manufactured this story. She was certainly quick-thinking, he'd give her that. She must have realized long before he did that they would have to work together because they were all guilty of heinous crimes, either this weekend or in the past – or both – and there was no stronger bond than a shared secret.

Helena

She had taken over the role of guide. Perhaps it was symbolic that she should take over her brother's job.

Ironically, the weather was excellent now and she navigated her way back easily to the lodge, though it was clear from their confusion about the route that neither Daníel nor Gunnlaugur would have had a chance on their own. The moors extended silent, white and featureless in every direction, and the going was heavy but not impossibly so.

The threat of mutually assured destruction made for a precarious balance within the group and so it would have to remain for the time being. All the secrets had been brought out into the open, all their dark sides.

She turned her mind resolutely away from Ármann. This wasn't the right time. But she couldn't even begin to imagine what life would be like without him at her side. They had been such a good team, complementing each other so well. He had been the man of action, letting his deeds speak for themselves, sometimes proceeding with more boldness than caution, and not always associating with the right people. But he had been a good person at heart, despite being capable of using violence when required. Above all, he had always looked out for her, his sister. Superficially, she had come across as more level-headed, cool and intelligent than him, but when the chips were down she was far more ruthless. At times he had turned to her when he was unsure what to do and she had generally chosen the right path, she thought, urging him never to back down, never to deviate from his plans. At other times he had gone off the rails, or taken on too much, and of course he'd come close to losing everything in Copenhagen, until she had intervened to save him.

Then recently she had found out, almost by chance, that Daníel had been with Víkingur on that fatal day. It hadn't taken her long to convince Ármann that this was a case of the old adage: an eye for an eye, a tooth for a tooth. The idea had been hers but Ármann had taken care of the planning.

That's how it had always been.

Yet despite their well-laid plans, the weekend had ended in disaster, with Ármann gone and Daníel still alive.

She had told Daníel it was time to bury the hatchet; that things had gone far enough, and from now on they would each go their separate ways and preferably never see each other again.

Glancing over her shoulder, she saw that he wasn't far behind, walking with his head down.

Unsurprisingly, he thought he had got away with it.

She would let him live with that illusion.

For a while.

COMING IN 2023

REYKJAVÍK

A THRILLING NEW MYSTERY FROM
RAGNAR JÓNASSON
AND ICELANDIC PRIME MINISTER
KATRÍN JAKOBSDÓTTIR

READ ON FOR A PREVIEW . . .

1956

6 August

The grey hat flew out to sea.

Kristján had stepped out of the wheelhouse to admire the view over Faxaflói bay and watch the island approaching, low and green against the backdrop of mountains. When the squall hit the little fishing smack, he had reacted fast but not fast enough, grabbing for his hat, only to snatch at thin air. Still, though he'd have never admitted it aloud, it could have been worse: the hat, a Christmas present from his wife, hadn't really suited him. Now he would have an excuse to buy a new one.

It meant he would be bare-headed for his visit to Videy, an island just off the Reykjavík coast. But what did that matter, when the whole thing was bound to be a waste of time? Despite having turned thirty, Kristján was rarely trusted with anything important. This time, though, his superior officer was on holiday – not far away, just in his summer cabin, a few kilometres outside Reykjavík – and Kristján had been asked to take the phone call.

Summer seemed like a distant memory that August

morning on the boat, with no shelter from the wind and the sun hidden by cloud. As there was no regular ferry service to the island, Kristján had had to improvise and do a deal with an old fisherman he knew.

'Almost there, Kristján,' the captain called from the wheelhouse, his voice hoarse.

Kristján nodded, though there was no one to see, and did up another button on his overcoat to keep out the cold. If nothing else, at least the trip made for a change of scene, he thought, trying to look on the bright side.

A woman, probably in her early thirties, was standing by the jetty to meet him. Kristján had asked his fisherman friend to come back for him in an hour and a half. The whole morning would go on this visit.

The woman held out her hand.

'I'm Ólöf Blöndal. Welcome to Videy.' Her face was grave, unsmiling.

'How do you do? The name's Kristján,' he said. There was something slightly off about Ólöf's manner, he thought. She looked a little shifty, yet at the same time he got the feeling she was relieved to see him.

He took in the fact that she had short red hair and was wearing a thick woollen jumper.

'It's this way,' she said, a little diffidently, and set off up the grassy slope from the jetty. He followed. Two striking white buildings with black roofs came into view: the old Danish colonial mansion, and the little church beside it. Halfway there, Ólöf stopped, turned and said: 'We're not actually going there. My husband's at home – we live nearby.'

Kristján nodded. 'Does nobody –?'

She interrupted: 'We have keys to the mansion but no one lives there. It's in pretty good nick, though, considering its age. It's almost two hundred years old, you know. The oldest stone building in Iceland.'

'This girl, Lára – '

Again she cut him off: 'It's best you speak to my husband.'

Kristján walked along beside her, neither of them saying a word. There was a blustery breeze blowing on the island but it was warmer than it had been on the crossing, despite the lack of sun. After they had been walking for a couple of minutes, he asked: 'Excuse me, but you said you live here, you and your husband?'

'We moved here in the spring last year; it's our second summer here. I have family links to Viðey. It's several years since anyone last farmed here but we've, um, we've been thinking of giving it a shot. It's . . .' She paused. 'There's nowhere quite like it.'

Kristján didn't doubt it; the island was certainly a picturesque spot, but Ólöf's words rang a little hollow to him.

She went on, awkwardly: 'It's not far to the house.' Though this was obvious.

It occurred to Kristján that he might have been sent to the island because of a misunderstanding. Although he was finding it hard to work this woman out, he didn't get the impression that there was some big mystery here that needed solving.

He let his mind wander. Being in the open air agreed with him, but he would rather have been spending this late summer's day doing something quite different. In recent years he and a couple of old friends had taken up mountaineering in their free time, inspired by the news three years earlier of Edmund Hillary and Tenzing Norgay's conquest of Everest. While Kristján had no hope of ever achieving those heights, he was making good progress. Only a few days ago news had come in that the north Icelandic peak of Hraundrangi in Öxnadalur had been climbed for the first time. Kristján was acquainted with the two Icelanders who had made the ascent along with an American. What he wouldn't have given to be there right now, rather than here in the tame environs of Videy.

Still, gentle though the terrain was, he was careful where he set his feet as he picked his way over the tussocky ground. He'd rather leave here without twisting or spraining an ankle – or dirtying his suit, for that matter. He owned three suits: this light-grey one was the newest; the pinstripe was looking a little threadbare these days, and the black one he saved mainly for formal occasions and funerals.

An old wooden house now appeared ahead, its black paint flaking. It had obviously seen better days. At that moment an Arctic tern swooped over Kristján's head and he made a grab for his hat to ward the bird off, only to remember belatedly that the hat was now floating somewhere in Faxaflói bay.

'Don't worry,' Ólöf said. 'The breeding season's over, so it won't attack you.' Her tone was momentarily lighter, as if she had forgotten that she was in the company of a policeman.

Her husband wasn't waiting outside the house for them. Noting this, Kristján wondered why it was Ólöf who had come to meet him off the boat. Was this the way the couple normally did things or could there be something else behind it?

'Come in,' Ólöf said rather curtly, once they reached the house.

Kristján entered a hall that turned out to be part of the sitting room. It was warm inside; almost uncomfortably so for the time of year.

'Óttar?' Ólöf called. 'Óttar, he's here.'

Kristján heard a noise upstairs, then footsteps boomed through the old wooden house. Ólöf didn't say a word, just walked into the sitting room and pulled out a chair from a large oak table, indicating that Kristján should take a seat.

He did so and waited. She sat down as well.

'Good morning,' said the man who had come down the stairs. 'I'm Óttar. I take it you're Kristján?'

'I am, indeed. Thank you very much for agreeing to meet me. I only managed to explain briefly over the phone, but, the thing is, we're worried about Lára.'

'She decided to leave,' Óttar said flatly. 'She gave up on her position here. I don't know why. We were so pleased with her at the beginning of the summer; she seemed hardworking and conscientious. Still, young people today . . .' His face was expressionless as he produced this speech. Kristján shot a glance at Ólöf, who dropped her gaze.

'How old was she again?' Kristján asked, though he already knew the answer.

'Fifteen,' Ólöf answered quietly.

'Fifteen,' Kristján repeated. 'And she'd decided to go back to Reykjavík, you say? Back home?'

'Yes,' Óttar replied.

'When?'

'On Friday. Friday morning. Naturally, I objected. We had an agreement that she would stay the entire summer as our help, but there was no talking any sense into her.'

Kristján glanced at Ólöf again. She was sitting tight, staring down at her hands.

'As I mentioned on the phone, no one's seen or heard from her in Reykjavík . . .' Kristján left the words hanging as he watched their reactions. Ólöf didn't raise her eyes; Óttar's face remained impassive.

'So, she left on Friday?' he prompted.

Óttar nodded.

'Maybe I should have put it differently: did you see her leave?'

'We can't see the jetty from here,' Óttar replied. 'And it was hardly my job to give the girl a send-off. If people want to leave, that's their business, as far as I'm concerned.'

'What about you, Ólöf? Did you see her go?'

Ólöf shook her head. 'I didn't see anything,' she said heavily.

'How was she intending to get back to town?'

'I have absolutely no idea. She said someone would be coming by boat – some friend or relative, I assume. I don't keep an eye on the boat traffic.'

'Are you sure she left?'

'What kind of question is that?' Óttar asked, bridling.

'Of course we're sure. She said goodbye and we haven't seen her since.'

Kristján looked at Ólöf, waiting for her to answer. She was silent at first, then said: 'Yes, she's definitely gone. She took her belongings with her.'

'Her parents used to hear from her regularly,' Kristján said, 'so when she didn't ring at the weekend, they started to get worried. Haven't they been in touch with you?'

'Yes, they certainly have,' Óttar replied. 'And I told them the same as I'm telling you. I simply can't understand why you've put yourself to the trouble of coming all the way out here. We could have answered your questions over the phone. You can see for yourself that the girl has gone.'

'I'd need to take a walk around the island to be sure on that point. Videy's quite large, isn't it?'

'One and a half square kilometres,' Óttar said.

'One point seven,' Ólöf corrected.

'And I expect there are a few hiding places?'

Ólöf said: 'Well, there's our house, and the mansion, of course. And the church. The old school too. And . . .'

'I don't think we need to list all the buildings on the island, Ólöf. Let the man do what he likes if he feels obliged to make sure. Though I can't imagine why on earth he thinks Lára would have been hiding somewhere on the island for the whole weekend.'

'How was she?'

'How do you mean?' Óttar asked.

'Was she in low spirits? Is there any reason to believe

she might have been hiding something? Keeping a secret from you?'

Óttar opened his mouth to answer, then seemed to think better of it. After a lengthy pause, he said: 'There was nothing wrong with the girl. She was simply bored of being here with us. Well, good riddance, I say. We'll be more careful when choosing our help next summer.'

'I see. At any rate, she hasn't turned up at her parents' place. Which raises questions, that's all. Of course, it's always possible she left here on Friday and – '

Óttar interrupted: 'Possible? I'm telling you, she left, and anything that happened after that has nothing to do with us. The boat didn't sink, so it stands to reason she must be somewhere.'

'No, I'm sure we'd have heard if something like that had happened,' Kristján said. 'The trouble is, there's no report of any boats coming out here on Friday, though that doesn't rule out the possibility that someone came and picked her up. Did she live here in the house with you?'

'Where else?' Óttar asked brusquely.

'Could I see her room?'

Óttar shrugged. 'It's upstairs. But there's nothing to see.' He showed no signs of budging but Ólöf rose to her feet.

'I'll take you up,' she said, her tone friendlier than her husband's.

Every stair creaked in the old wooden house. The guestroom was small but reasonably cosy, with a sloping ceiling, a bookcase and a dormer window with a view of the sea.

'Did she bring the books with her?' Kristján asked.

'Oh, no, those are ours. We put books in all the rooms. It's, well, it creates a nice atmosphere. My husband collects books. He's a barrister, as you're probably aware. Quite well known, actually.'

Kristján was indeed familiar with the name. He nodded.

'Óttar wanted to cut down on his legal practice and devote himself to academic work for a while. We're planning to try and live here more or less in the summers. It's good to be near ...' She trailed off, looking away. It seemed obvious to Kristján that she wasn't being entirely honest; that there was something more to it. Something more serious, he thought.

'Did she take all her belongings with her?' he asked.

'All of them, yes,' Ólöf said. 'There's nothing here.'

'Did she say anything to you?'

'I'm sorry?'

'Lára. Before she left?'

'What do you mean?'

'How did she explain her decision?'

Ólöf hesitated. 'She didn't explain,' she said eventually. 'She, er, she just left.'

'She must have said something before she left. According to your husband, she did.'

'Oh yes, I'm sorry. I didn't mean it like that. She just said she wanted to give up her position early. She asked our permission. Naturally, we granted it.'

'Aren't you worried about her?'

'Worried? What? No, we've only just learnt that she hasn't turned up at home. But I'm sure she's fine.'

'Let's hope so.'

'Shall we go back down?'

Kristján nodded and followed Ólöf down the narrow staircase.

When they entered the sitting room, Óttar was nowhere to be seen. Kristján looked around, then jumped when Óttar coughed behind him. He spun round, his heart beating uncomfortably fast, though of course he knew there was nothing to fear.

'There's a telephone call for you.'

'What?' Kristján exclaimed.

'There's a telephone call for you,' Óttar repeated, as though nothing could be more natural. 'In here – in my study.'

'Oh?' Puzzled, Kristján followed Óttar into the book-lined room. His eye fell on a shelf of volumes containing Supreme Court judgements. On the desk he saw a black telephone with the receiver lying beside it. There was a noticeable smell of mildew. It seemed the house was as dilapidated indoors as its outer appearance had suggested.

'Who's trying to get hold of me?' Kristján asked.

'Someone from the police, of course,' Óttar replied.

Kristján raised the receiver to his ear. 'Kristján Kristjánsson speaking.'

'Kristján, hello. Eiríkur here.' Kristján knew instantly who it was. The man was two rungs senior to him in the police: his boss's boss.

'Hello . . .' he replied diffidently.

'Óttar got in touch. He'd like an explanation for the, er, rather odd questions you've been asking him and his wife.'

'They were purely routine questions. I'm investigating the disappearance of a girl, a fifteen-year-old, who hasn't been seen for several days – '

'A girl who ran away from home, in other words?'

'Well, we can't be quite sure of that. She was in service here on Videy. Her parents are worr – ' He didn't get a chance to finish the sentence.

'There's no call to cause Óttar and Ólöf any unnecessary inconvenience over this. I gather you've gone to the trouble of visiting the island in person?'

Kristján wanted to protest, to try to explain, but reflected that it probably wouldn't do any good. 'Actually, I was about to leave. My visit here was just ending.'

'Excellent. Give Óttar my regards, would you? And Ólöf Blöndal too. You'll do that for me?'

Eiríkur hung up.

Kristján replaced the receiver carefully, trying to behave as if nothing had happened.

'Nothing urgent,' he told Óttar.

Ólöf was standing in the sitting room when they emerged from the study.

'Right, I think that's all for now. Unless you happen to have remembered anything else?' Kristján looked at the couple in turn.

'Nothing else,' Óttar replied for both of them.

'Then let's just hope the girl turns up,' Kristján said.

Óttar spoke for them both again. 'She's bound to. Not that it's any of our concern. I assume we won't be receiving any more visits like this.'

'Just one more thing,' Kristján said. 'The boat won't be

back to fetch me straight away. Would you mind if I took a stroll around the island while I'm waiting? Maybe I could have a look and see if she's hiding somewhere . . .'

'Hiding?' Ólöf echoed in surprise.

'Do as you please,' Óttar said. 'We don't own the island.'

'I think I'll go for a short walk, then. Thank you very much for your time.'

Kristján walked to the schoolhouse at the eastern end of the island. The trip there and back took longer than he'd expected. The schoolhouse was empty of course, with no sign that Lára had ever been there. It was the same story with the mansion.

Anxious not to keep the boat waiting, Kristján walked briskly back in the direction of the jetty. There was a fine view of Reykjavík on the opposite shore. The town was developing into a city, he reflected, with all those new neighbourhoods springing up and the imposing church gradually taking shape on the hill. In the end he reached the jetty early. The boat hadn't arrived yet, which gave him a chance to go back and take a quick look inside the island's little church. Although he knew he wouldn't find the lost girl there, he checked anyway.

The air was stale inside but the interior was impressive, despite its small size. It occurred to Kristján that this might be a good place to get married to Gudrún, though it was bound to be a palaver having to ferry the wedding guests to and fro. He would bear it in mind. He and Gudrún had been engaged for six months and were beginning to discuss the future, marriage and children. They lived in the west end of Reykjavík and Gudrún had recently started work at a grocery store there. Yes, maybe one fine day they would find themselves standing before the altar in here . . .

There weren't many hiding places in the small church, and, from the musty smell, he guessed the door hadn't been opened in a while. It could do with an airing.

When Kristján stepped outside again, he spotted the fishing boat in the distance, making steady progress towards the island.

Kristján walked slowly down to the jetty, trying to enjoy his outing in spite of having received what almost amounted to a dressing down from his superior. Completely undeserved, of course. Kristján was only trying to do his job, but people like Óttar and Ólöf had influential friends. And there wasn't much he could do about that.

Reaching the jetty ahead of the boat, he stood and waited. The sun was breaking free of the clouds now and the blustery wind that had greeted him was dying down to a gentle breeze. He gazed out across the bay, feeling a faint regret, after all, for the hat that had been snatched away.

His thoughts returned to the missing girl. She was probably holed up safe somewhere and her parents were making a fuss about nothing. It occurred to him that he didn't know what she looked like. He would have to ask for a photograph of her if she didn't turn up.

Yes, more likely than not she would be found safe and sound, and this would be his last trip to Videy for the foreseeable future. But as the old fishing smack came to rest against the jetty, Kristján had a powerful intuition that the case was far from closed.

DISCOVER MORE FROM

RAGNAR JÓNASSON